GABRIEL'S GIFT

· *a novel* ·

HANIF KUREISHI

Scribner

NEW YORK   LONDON   TORONTO   SYDNEY   SINGAPORE

SCRIBNER
1230 Avenue of the Americas
New York, NY 10020

First Scribner Edition 2001
Originally published in Great Britain in 2001 by Faber Limited

SCRIBNER and design are trademarks of
Macmillan Library Reference USA, Inc., used under license
by Simon & Schuster, the publisher of this work.

For information about special discounts for bulk purchases,
please contact Simon & Schuster Special Sales:
1-800-456-6798 or business@simonandschuster.com

Designed by Kyoko Watanabe
Text set in Sabon

Manufactured in the United States of America

1   3   5   7   9   10   8   6   4   2

Library of Congress Cataloging-in-Publication Data

Kureishi, Hanif.
Gabriel's gift : a novel / Hanif Kureishi.
p. cm.
1. Boys—Fiction. 2. Parent and child—Fiction. I. Title.
PR6061.U68 K87 2001
823'.914—dc21   2001042635

ISBN 0-7432-1711-X

For Kier

GABRIEL'S GIFT

One

"School—how was, today?"

"Learning makes me feel ignorant," said Gabriel. "Has Dad rung?"

As well as the fact he didn't know where his father was, something strange was happening to the weather in Gabriel's neighborhood. That morning, when he left for school with Hannah, there was a light spring shower, and it was autumn.

By the time they had reached the school gates, a layer of snow sat on their hats. At lunchtime in the playground, the hot floodlight of the sun—suddenly illuminated like a lamp—had been so bright the kids played in shirtsleeves.

In the late afternoon, when he and Hannah were hurrying home along the edge of the park, Gabriel became certain that the leaves in the park were being plucked from the ground and fluttered back to the trees from which they had fallen, before turning green again.

HANIF KUREISHI

From the corner of his eye, Gabriel noticed something even odder.

A row of daffodils were lifting their heads and dropping them like bowing ballerinas at the end of a performance. When one of them winked, Gabriel looked around before gripping Hannah's hairy hand, something he had always been reluctant to do, particularly if a friend might see him. But today was different: the world was losing its mind.

"Has he been in touch?" Gabriel asked.

Hannah was the foreign au pair.

"Who?" she said.

"My father."

"Certainly no. Gone away! Gone!"

Gabriel's father had left home, at Mum's instigation, three months ago. Unusually, it had been several days since he had phoned, and at least two weeks since Gabriel had seen him.

Gabriel determined that as soon as they got back he would make a drawing of the winking daffodil, to remind him to tell his father about it. Dad loved to sing, or recite poetry. "Fair daffodils, we weep to see / You haste away so soon . . ." he would chant as they walked.

For Dad the shops, pavements and people were alive like nature, though with more human interest, and as ever-changing as trees, water or the sky.

In contrast, Hannah looked straight ahead, as if she were walking in a cupboard. She understood little English and when Gabriel spoke to her she grimaced and frowned like someone trying to swallow an ashtray. Perhaps they were both amazed that a kid spoke better English than she did.

Although Gabriel was fifteen, until recently his father had usually walked him home from school in order to keep him away from any possible temptations and diversions. Not long ago Dad had had to rescue Gabriel from a dangerous scene in a nearby block of flats. Fortunately Dad was a musician and often had spare time during the day; too much spare time, said Gabriel's mother, who had started to find Rex himself somewhat "spare." Going to the school had been the only "structure" Dad had, apart from his daily visits to the pub, where several of the other parents also considered the world through the bottom of a beer glass.

Gabriel and his father often stopped at cafés and record shops. Or they went to collect the photographs Gabriel had taken recently, which were developed by a friend of Dad's who had a darkroom. In the sixties and seventies this man had been a successful fashion and pop photographer. The girls with ironed hair and boys in military jackets he had "immortalized," as he liked to put it, were as distant to Gabriel as Dickens's characters. The man was out of fashion himself and rarely worked; however, he liked to talk about photography, and he lent Gabriel many books and tore pictures from newspapers, explaining what the photographer had tried to do.

Dad liked to say that school was the last place where anyone could get an education. But outside, if your eyes were open, there were teachers everywhere. All that Dad recalled from his own school days was something about wattle and daub, freezing swimming pools at nine in the morning, and the rate of glacier movement, which was—well, he couldn't remember.

Getting home was a protracted business for Gabriel and his father. Planting his legs wide on the pavement and swinging his hand for illustration, Dad would ask the most intimate questions of people he knew only vaguely—How much do you drink? Do you still go to bed together? Do you love her?— which, to Gabriel's amazement, the person not only answered but elaborated on, often interminably, as Gabriel's father nodded and listened. The two of them would discuss the results for the rest of the way home.

Now Dad had gone and was living somewhere else. If the world hadn't quite been turned upside down, it was at an unusual and perilous angle, and certainly not still.

Since Dad's departure, Gabriel's mother insisted that Hannah pick Gabriel up. Mum didn't want to worry about him more than she already did.

Today, as Gabriel and Hannah rushed on, there was a sound behind them: it was either a giant clapping in their ears, or thunder. Going up the front path, a cloud of fog and hail descended and they couldn't see in front of them. Gabriel tripped on the step, but luckily Hannah was ahead of him. At least she guaranteed a soft landing.

When Gabriel returned from school these days, the house almost echoed. Neither of his noisy, quarrelsome parents came to the door. Normally he, Mum and Dad would have Earl Grey in a pot, crumpets soggy with butter—"I love a bit of crumpet in the afternoon," Dad would always say, a remark that could only have hastened his departure—and cakes; they loved anything involving cream and chocolate.

What had happened was this.

One evening, three months ago, Gabriel had looked out of the living room window and seen his father packing his clothes and guitars into the back of a friend's van. Dad returned to the house, kissed his son, and waved at him from the street.

Gabriel had run to the gate. "Where are you going?"

"Away," said Dad. "For a time."

"On tour?"

"I'm afraid not."

"On holiday?"

"No. No . . ."

"Where then?"

"Gabriel—"

"Is it my . . . er, bad behavior, that has caused this?"

"Could be . . . Oh, don't be stupid."

In a hurry to get away, and not wanting to talk, his father had stood there with his oldest guitar under one arm and a shaving bag, briefcase and trumpet under the other. For some reason he had a camera round his neck, as well as a bag out of which shirts were tumbling; his pockets were packed with underpants and socks; planted on his head were several woolly hats.

"Go inside," he said. "Keep warm."

"When are you coming back?"

"I will explain everything later," he said, as he always did when he intended to say nothing.

"Don't go." Gabriel took his hand. "Stay a bit longer. I won't interrupt when you're talking for a long time."

His father had pulled away. "I've got to get out. It's what your mother wants. Will you pick up those socks for me? You know I can't bend over."

Gabriel had stuffed the fallen socks into his father's top pocket. Dad climbed into the van.

As it started to draw away, Mum had raced from the house and flung at the van, with hysterical strength, a forgotten pair of Dad's boots which the car behind ran over, crushing them. When the van stopped and Dad climbed down to pick up his useless flattened footwear, Gabriel wondered whether his father might return to the house.

"My favorite part of that man is his back," Mum had said, slamming the door. "But what will happen now, I don't know. You never stop eating and wanting!"

"Me?" he said. This was normally how she talked to Dad.

"We haven't got any money!" she said.

"We'll have to earn some."

"What a good idea. When are you going to start work?" She looked at him properly. "In lots of ways you're still a little kid but actually you're big enough. But I wouldn't want you to put up with what I've been through."

The rumble and whirr of his mother's sewing machine had been the soundtrack to Gabriel's childhood. She had started off, in a more glamorous time, by making party clothes for her young, fab friends in the music business, and then for the bands, their managers and groupies. Mum had done it as a favor and because she liked to please. Had she been a designer like her heroine Vivienne Westwood, she might have progressed.

As it was, for the last few years she had supported herself, Gabriel and Rex by working in a cramped room in the house, making tour jackets for groups, roadies and their helpers. Sometimes she had to work all night for weeks to have them ready, doing everything herself, with only opera on the radio for company.

A few years ago, when the country decided it should become entrepreneurial and began dizzily to bolt about like someone who'd just awoken from an overlong sleep, she had tried to expand the business by renting a small warehouse and employing the unemployed. But the work had been irregular and she had got into debt. Now, working alone again, the job was lonely. She was looking for something else; somehow her whole life had become a "looking for something else."

Gabriel considered the ideas his parents used to enjoy discussing over supper. One of them was for a shop that sold only blue objects. Another was for a shop that sold pajamas.

"It isn't difficult to see why we haven't been able to afford a new carpet for years," Mum had said.

A better idea was for a shop where you could pop in to have your dreams interpreted and be told your future. Mum had said this wasn't entirely vapid: if you saw the present or the past in a dream, you could predict the future, since for most people the present was merely the past with a later date. Gabriel wasn't sure how lucrative this would be, even if dreams, like pajamas, were something that everyone had to have.

"At night even the most conservative of us becomes an avant gardist," his mother had said.

Gabriel had been very interested in this. "I want to be an avant gardist all the time," he said.

"That's why they have schools," said his father. "To stamp out that kind of thing."

His parents had argued a lot, saying the same things repeatedly, louder each time. He remembered his father placing objects in inconvenient positions on the floor, in the hope that Mum would fall over and break her neck.

It was clear that she, in her turn, wanted Rex to wake up one day as a different sort of person, the type who earned money, didn't mind cleaning, sometimes kissed her, and was less melancholic than her. A tall order, obviously.

Gabriel had never seen his mother more agitated than on the day his father left. She had gone into her room and shut the door. What could Gabriel do but sit outside trying to draw, waiting for her? It reminded him of standing on a chair at the window as a child, awaiting Mum's return from the shops.

"When I'm gone, you won't know what to do without me," Dad used to say.

"When you're gone, Rex, we'll know exactly what to do. Our souls will soar. You're the ballast in our balloon, mate. We'll be better off in every way," his mother replied.

Would they be?

He thought he heard his mother opening the window. Drawers were pulled out; the wardrobe door banged. For too long, there was silence. He wanted to call someone. But who? The police? A neighbor? Mum might stay in bed for days, perhaps for weeks. If she wasn't arguing with Father, what would she do?

He had noticed, in his friends' parents too, that there were different styles of madness for men and women, fathers and mothers. The women became obsessive, excessively nervous, afraid and self-hating, fluttering and blinking with damaged inner electricity. The men blunted themselves with alcohol and cursed, blamed and hit out, disappearing into the pub and then into jail.

When it came to suffering, Gabriel's mother was, at least

here, something of an artist, with a range of both broad and subtle maneuvers. She could enter an airless tunnel of silence that would wither Rex and Gabriel until they felt like dried sticks; or she could put together words and noises of a force that could fling them against a wall and leave them shaking for days. Whichever method she selected was guaranteed to ensure that her "common-law" husband and son felt it was them—bad guilty men, both—who had strangled and stifled her.

Waiting for her, the words "broken" and "home" had come to mind. "He's from a broken home," he recalled people saying of other children, with knowing pity. He pictured a drawing ripped in two, and a doll's house with an axe through it. He thought of how it felt to miss people and the relief of their return. With his father, though, it seemed to be an absence without end. Gabriel had never been angrier. It wasn't even as though he had been consulted. But what family was ever a democracy from the kids' point of view?

At last he had looked up. He would know what the future would be like.

The door had opened. His mother was wearing her darkest, most menacing clothes and makeup; her hair was scraped back.

"Get our coats."

"Are you going to get a new boyfriend?"

"I'll find a job first. It's time we got moving." As he hurried for their coats, she said, "I think you quite like all this exciting action."

"So do you," he said.

"Maybe," she said. "Now—into the future!"

That evening and the next morning she and Gabriel had gone to offices, shops and restaurants, asking, wheedling and arguing.

"Not you, I don't want to see you, but the boss!" Mum had said to the unfortunate person deputed to dismiss her.

This technique had been successful.

His mother had started work the following Monday, as a waitress in a fashionable new bar replete with armchairs, lamps and big windows, where young people could do what they enjoyed most: study themselves and one another in numerous mirrors. Like all the bars now, it was bathed in colored light, blue or red or pink.

"They asked me whether I'd had any experience," she had told him. "Experience, I said! I'm a mother and wife. I'm used to waiting on ungrateful, detestable people."

He had been to the bar but didn't like the way young people in polo necks, puffa-jackets and leather trousers snapped their fingers at her and shouted "Excuse me!" or "Waitress!" as she flew over the floor with tiers of dishes attached to her, looking as though she were trying to carry an open venetian blind. Now Gabriel crossed the road when he came to the place. At work, she was like a woman he used to know.

The new bar was an indication of either futile hope or a new direction. The city was no longer home to immigrants only from the former colonies, plus a few others: every race was present, living side by side without, most of the time, killing one another. It held together, this new international city called London—just about—without being unnecessarily anarchic or corrupt. There was, however, little chance of being understood in any shop. Dad once said, "The last time I visited the barber's I came out with a bowl of couscous, half a gram of Charlie and a number two crop. I only went in for a shave!"

Their neighborhood was changing. Only that morning a man had been walking down the road with a moldy mattress on his head, which you knew he was going to sleep on; other men shoved supermarket trolleys up the street, looking for discarded junk to sell; and there were still those whose idea of dressing up was to shave or put their teeth in.

However, there lived, next door, pallid television types with builders always shaking their heads on the front step. If you weren't stabbed on the way, you could find an accurate acupuncturist on the corner, or rent a movie with subtitles. In the latest restaurants there was nothing pronounceable on the menu and, it was said, people were taking dictionaries with them to dinner. In the delis, queens in pinnies provided obscure soups for smart supper parties. Even ten years ago it was difficult to get a decent cup of coffee in this town. Now people threw a fit if the milk wasn't skimmed to within a centimeter of its life and the coffee not picked on their preferred square foot of Arabia.

For those who knew, what really presaged a rise in house prices was the presence of film crews. Hardly a day passed without tangled wires on the pavement, people with clipboards wearing big jackets, numerous trucks, and fans, thieves and envious kids drawn by the self-importance of very little happening very slowly. Gabriel was one of those kids. To him the word "Action," preceded by the particularly intriguing "Turn over!," had a mesmeric effect. He couldn't wait to use these words himself.

Because his mother worked most of the day now, and often, in the evening, didn't come back until he was asleep, she wanted someone to keep an eye on Gabriel and look after the house. She had said to one of her women friends, "I'd no sooner leave a teenager alone than I would a two-year-old. In fact a teenager would get into more trouble!"

Hannah, a refugee from a former Communist country, was that restless eye, which slept, encased in the rest of her, on a futon in the living room.

"Why have you chosen her?" Gabriel had whisperingly inquired, the first time Hannah came to the house.

She was a big round woman, like a post-box with little legs, dressed always in widow black.

"Unlike you, she's incredibly cheap to run," was the reply. "What were you expecting?"

"Julie Andrews, actually. Hannah's fat."

"I know." She was laughing. "But make friends with her. If you let yourself get to know people, you might come to like them."

"Is that right?"

"Please try and help me, Gabriel. I've never been through such a difficult time. I want us to have a good life again."

He had to promise to try. But his mother didn't trust him and she could have; she seemed to take pleasure in punishing him, as if she wanted to hurt everyone around her for what had happened.

Hannah was, as far as Gabriel was able to make out, from a town called Bronchitis, with a winding river called Influenza running through it. She had been recommended to them by a friend, or perhaps the person was secretly their enemy. Whatever the situation, when Hannah came to them with her Eastern European clothes and cardboard suitcase, she had nowhere else to live.

Mum had explained, in her practical way, "Hannah, you will have to sleep in the living room. But at least you will have accommodation, a little pocket money, and as much as you can eat."

The words—"as much as you can eat"—had proved to be unwise.

Hannah, whose only qualification with children was the possibility that she might once have been a child herself, at least knew how to eat. When she first arrived in England after spending three disoriented days in a coach admiring the motorways of Western Europe, she would walk around those heavens called supermarkets, twisting with desire and moaning under her breath like someone who had pushed a door marked Paradise rather than Tesco. To her, what people threw away would be a banquet.

Hannah could eat for England; she saw any amount of food

in front of her as a challenge, a food mountain to be scaled, swallowed, flattened. Once, Gabriel found her squeezing a tube of tomato puree down her throat.

Sometimes, to tease Hannah, Gabriel would say, "If you could choose to have anything in the whole world to eat, what would it be?"

"Ice cream," she would say in her strange accent. "Um . . . and burgers. Pigs' trotters. Pies. Rabbit stew. Jam. And . . . and . . . and . . ."

As she described her favorite meals, electric-eyed, lips moist and chest heaving, Gabriel would sketch the food. She would laugh at the drawings and pretend to eat the paper. Once he drew a picture featuring her several chins, inserting a zip into one, with half a sausage extending from it, a drop of mustard and smear of mayonnaise on the tip. This offended and upset her.

What she did like was Gabriel photographing her "in London," as she put it. Recently Gabriel had been taking photographs with cheap, disposable cameras which he used like a notebook. He liked to photograph odd things: street corners; people from behind; lampposts; shop fronts. He took Polaroids and drew on them with a pen. He didn't like anything too designed, too careful or artificial. Some of the pictures his father's friend had blown up onto large sheets, which Gabriel drew and painted on.

Gabriel had noticed that whenever he picked up a camera, Hannah became watchful and would wipe her crumby mouth, plump her split ends and adjust her collar. The pictures he did take, she sent home to her family. She was quite nice to him afterwards.

Mum knew it wasn't much fun with Hannah. At first Gabriel had refused to walk home with her. It wasn't just that he was too old to be walked home; he didn't want the others to know he had an "au pair." In some schools the middle class—to which Gabriel almost, but not quite, belonged—was a persecuted minority, and anyone who had the misfortune to come from such a minority did all they could to disguise it. They were so loathed, the members of this class, they even had their own schools. Luckily, there were several entrances to Gabriel's school and he could elude Hannah altogether, or just run away. But his mother became so upset that he compromised by having Hannah meet him not outside the school but on the corner; she walked home behind him. "I think that woman's following us," his friends would say.

"She's one of the local madwomen," Gabriel would say. "Ignore her."

However, she always had crisps and drinks for him, and as they neared the house and his friends went in different directions, he and Hannah would end up together.

As compensation, and to show off the benefit of her wage packet, Mum had taken him to see the Who—her favorite band—up the road at the Shepherd's Bush Empire. Mum still knew someone from the old days connected to the band, and they had great seats in the front of the circle. "I hope it's going to be loud," Mum had said, as they went in. It was. Afterwards, they had gone out to supper with their ears still numb. It seemed a long time ago.

Now Gabriel sat at the table eating his tea.

"I'll watch him, Mum," Hannah had promised. "Don't you worry, like a vulture I will observe the bad boy."

She did watch him; and he watched her watching him. Hannah had a queer look, for her eyes, instead of focusing on the same point in the normal way, pointed in different directions. He wondered if she might be able to watch two television programs simultaneously, on different channels, on each side of the room.

What she could certainly do was watch TV and keep an eye on him at the same time, while pressing boiled sweets into the tight little hole beneath her nose. To "improve my English" as she put it, she watched Australian soap operas continuously, so that her few English sentences had a Brisbane accent.

Even if Gabriel wasn't doing anything wrong, one of her eyes hovered over him. His mother must have given Hannah an unnecessarily prejudiced report of the scrapes and troubles he was prone to. But to Hannah, being a kid in the first place was to be automatically in the wrong and these wrongs—which were going on all the time—had to be righted by adults who were never in the wrong since adults were, all the time, whatever they did, the Law. Perhaps her experience of Communism had given her this idea. Wherever she had obtained it, she would prefer it if Gabriel didn't move at all, ever again. She liked it best when he wasn't there but was somewhere else, preferably asleep and not dreaming.

She loved food, but the meals she cooked tasted of dirty dishcloths and toenails, topped with a blood and urine sauce. Gabriel considered picking up the plate and flinging it at the wall. The pasta would, at least, make a pretty shape on the yellow wallpaper.

It had been his policy to be horrible to Hannah in the hope that he would drive her away and his mother would look after him again. But if he made a mess, Hannah would make him clear it up. If he sulked, she didn't notice; if he whined, she turned the TV up louder.

He pushed his plate away. Today Gabriel had an idea.

"Hey!" said Hannah.

"French homework. *Vous comprendez?* If Dad phones, you'll call me, won't you?"

"If I am available."

"Available?" He was laughing. "What else might you be doing?"

"Mind your own nose," she said, tapping her forehead. "He won't call anyway. He gone for good."

"No, Hannah. You don't know him. You've never met him."

"I won't met him."

"I'd watch what you say. He was a friend of the Rolling Stones. He played with Lester Jones, actually! His eyes get big and he shakes. He might come back and bite you somewhere you won't like."

"Bah!"

He picked up his school bag, fetched some other things from his own room, and went into his mother's bedroom.

His mother had always been tiresomely strict about his homework. She didn't want Gabriel to fail at school, for fear he would become an artist. Having spent her life among musicians, singers, songwriters, clothes designers and record producers, she knew how few of them had country houses with recording studios and trout farms. Most were on the dole, passing through rehabs, smelling of failure or dying of disappointment. It wasn't only lack of talent, though most were prodigiously untalented, with stupidity coming off them like bad charisma. Few had the basic ability to organize and preserve the proficiency they did have. When she was in a good mood, his mother said humorously that she didn't want to discourage Gabriel's artistic endeavor but crush it altogether, so he'd go into business, or become a doctor or lawyer able to support her in her "old age."

For a moment Gabriel stood at the window, wondering whether someone he knew might be walking up the street. He closed his eyes, hoping that when he opened them the person might appear. It was turbulent: clouds sailed past, as if being tugged by invisible strings; the sun and moon sat side by side in the sky, flashing on and off. All the weather seemed to be coming at once. Perhaps, when this strange period ended, there would be no climate at all but an enormous blankness.

His mind seemed to have turned into one of the psychedelic records his father used to play, closing his eyes and moving his arms like hypnotized snakes. This was a mystery tour he couldn't stop.

He pulled the curtains and climbed up to his mother's bed, which, to make more space in the high-ceilinged room, was on legs, with a little ladder up to it, and a table and chair under it. There was a padlocked metal drawer in the base of the bed, full of old cosmetics. On a shelf beside the bed was a pile of small and large art books he loved to look at. His mother had used them a long time ago, at art school. The books smelled musty but it was a seductive perfume. Within were worlds and worlds. Unlike films, they didn't move; he could get lost inside the colors and shapes.

He wondered what talking to the people would be like. Van Gogh's friendly looking postman, no doubt smelling of tobacco, seemed like someone to give lengthy advice. Degas's dancers, standing in a big ornate room with a churlish teacher waving a cane in front of them, seemed like girls he could take an interest in. One of the warm, pink dancers seemed to reach out to take his hand.

Gabriel had brought his sketchbook into his mother's room, along with the old pencil box with iron corners that his father had given him just before he left home, made up of drawers for pens, trays for rubbers and pencil sharpeners, and a hidden section that so far had nothing in it.

In the last few days he had been drawing the storyboard for a short film. He and his father had been watching Carol Reed's *Oliver!,* which, when Gabriel was younger, had been one of his favorites. The "Dodger" had been his original punk hero. At the annual school concert, Gabriel's version of "Consider Yourself," done in ripped tails, top hat, muddy boots and orange-tinted shades, had been much applauded by the junkies, pedophiles, no-hopers and greedy bastards called parents. Gabriel had thought it was still possible to make a film about the parts of London that most people never saw.

His idea was for a story called "Dealer's Day," about a young drug courier who is used by his older brother to make deliveries, and eventually gets caught and sent to a "secure" institution.

Gabriel was saving up to get a 16mm film camera, but that would take time. He would have to find lights and buy film stock. He would not use cheap video. His best friend Zak, a natural exhibitionist who fancied himself as an actor and singer, a boy who took it for granted that he would be successful, would play the lead; local kids would play extras and help with equipment. Gabriel wanted to make the film soon, before Zak was too old to play the kid.

Meanwhile, as he could see the film in his mind but was afraid of forgetting parts of it—once he started work new ideas occurred every day, often in a rush and usually on his way to school, where they faded like hidden murals exposed to the light—his father suggested he draw it. Dad had taken him to buy storyboards, books consisting of rows of white squares, like film frames, into which you could draw the scene. Beneath the pictures Gabriel neatly wrote the dialogue and had persuaded his father to start writing the soundtrack.

Lately he had done virtually nothing. Since Dad had left, it wasn't that Gabriel had lost concentration, for this came and went, like everything; it was that his sense of purpose was wavering. His father's interest had worked as a little driving motor. Why would anyone think they could achieve something? Only because someone believed in them.

Gabriel's grandfather—Dad's father—had been a greengrocer, with a shop in the suburbs. He had spent his days serving others, of whom he had a high opinion. Anyone who walked into his shop was better than him. He was a tight-lipped man from a generation who believed you "spoiled" children by being pleasant to them; you certainly shouldn't praise them. So convinced had he been by this that he had taken no interest in his son whatsoever. Dad felt he had been held back by this "small" idea of himself. He didn't want his son to be the same.

Gabriel thought of his father climbing into the van and being driven God knows where. This incident replayed itself repeatedly in his mind like a song that wouldn't go away. He remembered his mother crying in this room, his parents' bedroom, emptied now of his father's guitars, tablas and other musical instruments.

He thought, too, of the time, a few months ago, when his father had come to look for him after Gabriel had started to hang out in the local flats.

His mother had been working hard in her room and Dad had at last managed to get a job playing sixties songs in a bar in Oslo, sitting on a stool surrounded by blondes, going "Rebel, rebel, you're a star . . ."

After school, Gabriel had been meeting with some older and more "advanced" adolescents who had taken over a flat—known as the "drum"—in a nearby block. The place was filled with stolen junk like black and white TVs which the local fences couldn't pass on in neighborhood pubs.

The kids watched satellite TV with Bullseye, the albino Alsatian, and whisperingly busied about with much secret urgency, laboring at the most desirable alchemy known to mankind: how to earn money without getting a job. It wasn't too difficult. Many eleven-year-olds turned up after school, wearing Tommy Hilfiger coats over their uniforms, to buy hash. The demand was so great that an older kid had set up a counter in the kitchen called "the tuck shop," from behind which blocks of dope were handed over, like putrid chocolate bars.

A few street beggars came by, too—local kids, and children blown down from the North, who mostly slept in children's homes and hostels. Not only were they more experienced than Gabriel, but they had lived under harsh, cruel regimes. Terrible things had happened to these unprotected children, and, Gabriel guessed, somehow always would.

Despite his normalcy, or because of it, Gabriel was sent on

errands to flats, squats and street corners, delivering packages that he hid in his underwear and shoes. Being a "tiddler," and young and white, and knowing the local shortcuts and hideouts, he was less likely to be stopped by the police, or worse—other gangsters. Sometimes on these trips he pushed the prams of locals girls. Later he was told that the baby's nappies had been stuffed with sachets of uplifting powder.

Unlike some of the other kids his age, he had never had a regular girlfriend. But there was a sex room in the drum. A couple of girls were so amused by his virginity that as a favor they had pushed him onto the dirty mattress and stolen his cherry, taking it in turns to hold a crying baby while the short, absurd ceremony continued.

"You won't forget that—buoy," one of them had said.

"No, I don't think I will," he had replied.

When Gabriel's father returned from Norway and failed to find him, he called at Zak's and other school friends of Gabriel's. No one had seen the boy. Asking everywhere for his son, Dad visited shebeens where sixties reggae was played over card games—there were towering piles of money on the tables and a threatening unease; he visited community centers where he heard "lovers' rock," and pool halls full of bejewelled gangs and posses in "pukka" gear.

Gabriel remembered Dad walking into the filthy drum, coming over to pick him up from the floor, and trying to heave him over his shoulder as if he were a child.

"I can walk," Gabriel had said. "You'll ruin your back again."

Dad had been carrying a guitar, and one of the older boys thought he was a tube busker looking for a score or a place to sleep. Gabriel giggled to himself at the thought of how irked his father would have been had he known this.

Gabriel had been impressed by how his father hadn't been afraid; he would have known that the kids were contemptuous of authority and carried knives and worse. But Gabriel saw, as his father touched fists with the kids and sat down to talk with them, that Dad didn't believe they were beyond his human reach.

When Dad led Gabriel away and told him never to return, saying he was too young for such a forlorn and unhappy place, Dad himself was troubled by the prohibition. He had grasped that Gabriel required other worlds and needed to move away from his parents. The "drum" was something Gabriel should know about, Dad said, but he didn't think, at the moment, that Gabriel could come through it intact. Some people felt compelled to live self-destructive lives, but these lives could become addictive and impossible to escape.

Dad had ridden to the rescue at the right moment: a grille for the drum door was arriving, and older, more serious villains were starting to use the place as a hideout. A few weeks later Gabriel heard at school that the "drum" had been raided, the police forcing everyone to lie on the floor. Some of the kids had been hauled out, smacked hard in the stomach and taken away. There were many available crimes for them to be fitted to.

After this, Gabriel was at home most of the time and his trespasses—horrid though they were—were mostly of the imagination. Fortunately there were plenty of them, since his mother, clearing out her room, had inadvertently made him a great gift. She had leaned a gilt-edged mirror against the wall at the end of his bed.

Looking in it one wet-fingered day after school, he had fallen in love. There would be a lifetime of such swooning! He understood why grown-ups whispered and what there was to hide. There was a secret. The world was a façade. It was the beyond, behind and underneath—a nether factory making dreams and stories that writhed with strange life.

He went to work.

In the glass-walled world, listening to music by Lester Jones,

Gabriel liked to watch himself smoking a cigarette in a kooky hat and exotic waistcoat, as if he were a movie character. Adjusting the angle of the mirror, he could pretend to be someone else, any woman he wanted to be or have, particularly if he had painted his toenails in some dainty shade and was wearing his mother's rings, necklaces and shoes. He preferred the ones with straps and heels, or anything that resembled a cross between a dagger and a boat. Low-heeled sandals did nothing for him. Perhaps they were an acquired taste. His mother, to his chagrin, didn't wear boots any more.

When he was in the "shoe" mood, the different characters he brought together enacted rumbustious scenes as he tore in and out of the mirror's eye, a crowd of actors in one body. It wasn't an uncreative pastime. If, like all children, he was a pervert, he was also a film director and screenwriter.

Today, however, he wasn't in a "shoe" mood. Earlier he had thrown a sheet over the mirror. He wanted to draw. A thought had remained in his mind from watching TV the other night. As far as he could remember, it went something like this: art is what you do when other people leave the room.

Left in his mother's room, he turned the pages of the art book until something attracted his attention.

He found himself looking at a picture of a pair of boots— gnarled, broken, old work boots. Often, when he wanted to draw, he copied something, to warm up. He decided to work in charcoal. As he sketched, the boots came easily, the lines seeming to make themselves in the way his legs did when running, without persuasion.

After a few minutes he noticed an unusual smell. He went to the door to see if Hannah was standing outside the room, as she was a person around whom different odors seemed to congregate, like bums on a street corner. He could hear her moving about downstairs in the kitchen. Probably she was dyeing her hair, which she did at least once a fortnight: this involved her putting a plastic bag on her head, which didn't stop strings of dark color running down her face, until she resembled a Christmas pudding.

No; the smell wasn't her.

Turning around, he saw that in the middle of the room were the boots he had copied from the book.

He walked around them, before going closer and squatting down. They smelt of dung, mud, the countryside and grass.

He picked the boots up, touched them, slipped off his shoes and tried them on, shuffled a little way, and collapsed. He couldn't stop laughing in surprise and perplexity. When he tired of this, he returned to the sketchbook. In the center of the page was a boot-shaped hole. As he turned the page, the boots were sucked back onto it, and everything returned to normal.

Or did it?

He looked about fearfully. An eerie terror, like a ghost, had swished into the room. The purple knob of the wardrobe handle seemed like one of Hannah's eyes. Perhaps it had detached itself from her face and flown up here to spy. He was reminded of a picture by Marc Chagall that featured a barn-like house with a huge all-seeing brown eye in the roof. When Gabriel returned the stare, the eye turned back into a dull rough surface.

He was disturbed but excited by what he'd done. It didn't seem like a dangerous ability. But it was wrong to mess with magic, wasn't it? He didn't know. Who would know? Parents and teachers were there to be believed in, or at least argued with. If they no longer functioned, or, like his father, were blasted by doubt, where was there to turn for the rules? Who knew what was going on?

He did what he always did at times like this: consulted his twin brother, Archie, truly his other half.

There would today—if fate hadn't fingered one of them—be two identical boys sitting side by side in this room, one born a few breaths later, clutching the heel of the other. Gabriel would be talking to, and looking at, himself and not-himself, face to face with his own features, worn by another.

Instead, the dead brother, alive inside the living half, had become a magic, and wiser, boy—Gabriel's daemon or personal spirit.

Gabriel's father still talked of how proud he had been, pushing his two sons up a hill in the tank of a double pushchair, face into the wind, to the park. Wherever he went with them, they drew crowds and comment. "Two for the price of one," he would say, standing back so others could look at, converse with or tickle his boys. "Double trouble," he'd add fondly.

Then, aged two and a half, one boy died from meningitis. It was a miracle, the doctors said, that the other survived.

How could Gabriel and his parents ever recover? For a long time he had been an imprisoned prince, living with an elusive woman who had gained a child and lost one. She could be both indifferent and passionate. He had never learned how to convert the one into the other, except in his imagination, where he could do anything, apart from be with other people; that was, he guessed, the hardest art of all.

When Gabriel was four, he almost drowned in the sea, his father running in to save him. At this, Mum almost drowned in sadness and terror herself. Afterwards, she had become too careful with Gabriel, not letting him live for fear he might die. Worry was like an engine that kept people alive. Fortunately, her husband had a reckless, frivolous streak, which stopped them all from suffocating, but she had entered a zone of fear that she was unable to leave. When he was young, they rarely left the house.

Gabriel didn't remember Archie outside of the many photographs of the twins together, displayed in the hall, his parents' bedroom and the living room. These precious framed pictures were never touched, moved or commented on, but they had always disturbed Gabriel for one important reason. His parents didn't know which boy was which. His mother claimed that, when Archie was alive, they and they alone could tell the two apart. But recently his father had admitted that he had given one boy a dose of medicine twice, and that sometimes they put them in the wrong cots and didn't realize the mistake until the morning.

This made Gabriel wonder whether they had been permanently mixed up. Perhaps he was Archie and Gabriel was dead. Certainly, he was always aware of his brother's absence, and whenever he saw a pair of twins he wanted to rush over and tell them or their mother that there were two of him, too; it was just that one of them was a shadow.

"Will Archie come back?" he liked to ask Mum, from the age of six. They had gone to visit his grave, as they always did on the anniversary of his death. Gabriel's birthday—their birthday—was always sad, too.

"No," she would say sharply. "Never, never."

"Does he hear us talking about him?"

"No."

"Does he think?"

"No."

"Does he see?"

"No."

"Not even black?"

"No. He sees nothing. Nothing for ever."

"Is he in heaven as well as under the ground?"

"He could be. Gabriel—"

"With his friends?"

"Gabriel, we carry him with us, wherever we go, in our minds but he will be dead for ever and ever and ever."

She would say no more and would clench and unclench her fists as if trying to retain water in the palm of her hand.

If Archie was in his mind, Gabriel always had someone to talk to. Together, the boys could conspire against their parents.

If Gabriel didn't fidget and listened carefully he could hear Archie, for Archie looked out for his brother and was sensible and always knew what to do. Sometimes, if he felt frivolous, Gabriel would call up Archie by singing "Two of Us" by the Beatles.

Now Gabriel became silent so as to hear his brother's voice whispering within his body.

Archie was saying not to be afraid; Gabriel should go on drawing. If the objects became real, it wasn't bad or black magic, just an unusual gift that could be of use. When Gabriel hesitated, Archie said that things might change, but that he should go on to see what might happen.

First, though, Gabriel would have to see if it might be possible to repeat the strange exercise.

On the next page of the art book was a picture of a yellow chair. He didn't want to admit liking this kind of art, just right for the front of a postcard. He'd rather prefer the stronger stuff: toilets, blood and pierced eyeballs with titles like "Pulsations of the Slit." The pretty pictures that had so shocked people in the old days had lost their power. But this one spoke to him now.

It was, as Archie murmured, useful. There was no point being snobbish. Their father, who had plenty of curiosity but little taste, except in music, might like it. The last time Dad had rung, he said he'd found somewhere to live. He had taken a room in a big house not far away.

"It's a little bare and cold," he had said. "But there's a bed and—"

"And?"

"Wardrobe."

What he needed were some bright pictures.

"What did he say? What did he say?" asked Gabriel's mother, who had fortuitously overheard the conversation, no doubt by bending over and pressing her ear to the door.

"Dad's found a room."

"What sort of room?"

"It's bare and cold."

"Oh dear." Mum had giggled. "Very cold? But he hates the cold."

"He hasn't got anywhere to sit."

He imagined his father standing up to read, eat and watch television, or leaning against the wall now and again, for relief.

As Gabriel started to copy the chair, he began to feel he was bringing it into existence. He worked rapidly; it was like singing a song: once you'd started you shouldn't think about it. When he had finished drawing and coloring in, he closed his eyes and looked up.

There it was.

He ran his hand over its ridges and curves. Gingerly, wondering whether it might collapse, he sat down. It was secure and comfortable. Gabriel stood on it, and danced a bit. It took his weight; this was a chair you could put your arse on and wiggle about.

When he returned to his sketchbook and turned the page, the real chair disappeared, but his copy remained.

The more he considered what he had done, the more disturbing he found it. Winking daffodils had tried to communicate with him. Dead brothers spoke within him. The earth, surely, had tilted and was trembling on its axis. Who would put it back before it tipped into eternity?

To check that everything else was as he'd left it, he went down to the living room to find Hannah watching television, her wayward eyes flickering fitfully in the darkening room.

"Hannah."

She looked about in surprise. "Bah!"

"What?" he said, grateful, almost, to hear another human voice.

"Bath!"

"Right."

She ran his bath.

He could do it himself but he liked her to feel capable. Really, the poor woman, of all people, was only his mother's conscience. Sometimes he wondered whether he thought about Hannah more than she thought about him.

She was watching him. "Those clothes—to me give."

"What will you do with them?"

"Wash."

"Hannah . . ."

"No, you mama says—three days too long without washing clothes. Every day you change clothes—she has ordered."

"You know it takes me a few days to start feeling comfortable in anything. Thinking about new clothes makes me feel tired. And I haven't got a girlfriend at the moment."

"Here!"

He put on a dressing gown and handed her his clothes. "Still, as Dad says, never wear anything that is actually stiff. Hannah, he's a funny guy."

"He is?"

"You should hear him. You'll understand when you meet him some time."

"You mama say, he is fool."

"What? She's a fool to say that."

Scowling, Hannah fetched clean towels.

He locked the door, bathed quickly and went to his room to do more "homework." When Hannah had checked on him and gone back to watch television, he crept into his mother's room. He picked up the art books from the floor, and looked and thought, afraid he might cry.

He had no idea what time his mother would come home; he had given up waiting for the hiss and rustle of her clothing, the trail of her perfume, the swing, fall and tickle of her hair, and her arms around him, pulling him into her. Samuel Beckett, whose play he had seen at school, produced by the local college, had been on to something: waiting was hard, wearing work, probably the worst torture of all, turning people into both victims and murderers in their minds.

Since his father had left and she had got a job, Mum had changed in other ways. For a start she had acquired a new wardrobe.

Late at night, when she came in to kiss him, she would wear a big fur-collared overcoat, jewellery and high heels. She would be accompanied by a symphony of new smells: the night air of unfamiliar parts of the city—he believed he could smell the East End on her at times, as well as aftershave, alcohol and marijuana. She had even, late in the evening, brought men he hadn't met into the house. Loud music would be played, bottles would be emptied, and there'd be dancing. In the morning she'd forget who he was and call him "Sugar."

Now, back in his bedroom, lying in the dark, he heard the door open slowly. He was afraid; it had been too strange a day already.

"Gabriel . . ." whispered Hannah. "Are you in this world?"

"At the moment."

"Something to tell."

"Mum's going to be even later?"

"Your dadda has ringed."

"Dad? It was him?"

"Yes."

"Didn't he want to speak to me?"

"He offer a message to say he will pick you up tomorrow."

"He's coming here?"

"He taking you to him place."

"To his house for the night? Is it that Mum's given permission?"

"Yes."

"Did he say what has happened to him? Is he all right?"

"No. No more enquiry. Pack your vest and underpant."

It would be the first time he had stayed with his father. Gabriel had been hoping for this.

"Sleep well," said Hannah. "Peace for me, tomorrow then."

"Get lost."

"What?"

"An English expression: may you get lost in sweet dreams."

"I get. Thanks. Get lost to you and God bless you fresh cheeks all night."

"And all your fresh cheeks, Hannah."

Two

After school the next day Gabriel was waiting at the living room window with Hannah behind him. He shut his eyes, and when he opened them his father was at the gate.

"Yes!" Gabriel shouted. "Yes, yes!" He turned to Hannah. "See, he did come."

"No noise," said Hannah. She was watching Dad warily.

Even though he knew Gabriel's mother was out at work, Dad didn't come into the house but stood on the step with his back to the door, tapping his foot as Gabriel packed his drawing things and art books into his rucksack.

Dad was unshaven, wore dark glasses and had his woollen hat pulled down. Gabriel remembered Mum saying to him, "Careful: people will take you for a burglar. A police record is the only recording you're going to make!"

"I'll burgle your arse in a minute!" he had replied, grabbing her.

On good days he would be affectionate, always touching, kissing and hugging. But Mum said he was clumsy, and didn't know how to touch.

Under his hat Dad was balding; the hair he did have was pulled back by a rubber band he picked up off the street. The rest was straggly and frizzy. His jeans were ripped—"ventilation" he called it—and he wore plimsolls, which gave him "uplift." His idea of dressing up was to pull a fresh pair from a number of similar boxes he kept in the cellar.

"Let's get going," Dad said, hurrying Gabriel away from the house.

Hannah stood at the window, mouthing, "Get lost!"

Gabriel said, "I've been excited all day. Two houses instead of one. I'll be like other kids now."

Gabriel was thinking of children whose absent parent felt so guilty they became eternally indulgent, and couldn't stop giving them presents.

"It's a kind of flat, not a house," said Dad.

To Gabriel's surprise they didn't go straight to Dad's place, but to the V&A in South Kensington, walking around the old jars and pots in an agitated silence that Dad called "meditative."

Gabriel was used to his father taking him to see the latest work—the strangest stuff—by young artists working in squats, lofts and abandoned garages. Gabriel had looked at heads made of blood, hair and old skin; he had seen dissected animals and strange photographs of body parts. The only canvas he saw was Tracy Emin's tent. Gabriel had learned that anything could be art. His father had no shame about knocking on the door of young artists he admired and going in for "a chat," since he knew they had been keen to talk about their work. Today, however, he wasn't feeling "inquisitive."

Gabriel had started to draw seriously two years before, when his father hardly worked and was at home much of the time. There were no artists in the family, but perhaps Gabriel had turned to art and making films because it wasn't something Dad had ever thought of doing.

Unlike most musicians, Dad could read music as well as play several instruments pretty well. The house had been full of guitars; Dad also used to have a saxophone, a piano and a drum kit. At one time, in a garage nearby, he had started to build his own harpsichord.

From the age of fourteen, Dad had played in many long-haired, short-haired and now, mostly, bald bands. He could play in any style, and sing in only one. Gabriel's mother called him Johnny-about-to-be-famous. Dad was smart enough to know that by his age you had either become successful, rich and pursued by lawyers, stalkers and the press, as some of his former friends had been, or you found something else to do. "Something else," of course, was an admission of failure; "something else" was the end.

Worse than this, according to Mum, was to play pool in the pub every day with other "superannuated long-hairs in dirty jeans," saying how the latest "beep-beep" music wasn't a patch on Jimi's or Eric's. This group of has-beens, who, as Gabriel once quipped, could hardly manage "joined-up talking," only left the pub to attend AA meetings. Mum, who remembered being at the center of the rock scene, wouldn't have these bums in the house. At night Dad went to his mates' houses to drink, jam and smoke dope.

At least Dad had never stopped loving music. It was just that he didn't get paid for it.

He still played live with these friends, in pubs or at parties and weddings, where no one listened and middle-aged people danced without moving their bodies. Not long ago they had been invited to play in a hotel while the guests had supper. It was a pretentious place but seventies music had been requested. Gabriel had gone along to help set up, as most of the band were in such bad shape they could barely lift their instruments.

Dad's band had played the tunes that millions had liked when he had been in Lester Jones's group, but one by one the guests were driven like refugees from the dining room, carrying their plates and some of them still chewing, until only one red-faced old man remained, dancing in front of the band. He danced till he collapsed into the arms of a doctor who was staying there.

Sometimes Dad became dejected, or distraught with envy at the young kids, not much older than Gabriel, who flashed across the nation's televisions, into the charts and *Hello!* magazine, and then were gone, carrying a good deal of money with them, if they were lucky.

Gabriel had played both guitar and piano from a young age and had been in a school group, playing indie rock, for a few weeks. He couldn't write songs and didn't improve as a musician. The pained look on his father's face—Dad hated him to play badly—made murder more likely and learning impossible. It was easier for Gabriel not to play, and, anyhow, Dad hated anyone touching his instruments. If Dad watched Gabriel, it was because he was worried about whether the boy would drop his best guitar. When, to the relief of them both, Gabriel "retired," what he did miss was having something big to be interested in.

One day his mother had taken him to see an exhibition of old and new drawings at the British Museum. Afterwards, she bought him pencils and a sketchbook. Like his father, Gabriel soon had his own "sacred" objects, obtained cheaply from the numerous secondhand shops in the area: paintbrushes, pencils, videotapes, old Kodaks. He started to take his "objects" wherever he went, in his special rucksack. If he placed something like a pencil or camera between himself and the world, the distance, or the space, enabled good ideas to grow. He and his father were working in parallel, rather than in competition.

When the weather was good and Dad was feeling "inquisitive," Gabriel and Dad used to ride their bicycles along the river. Dad refused to leave London: for him, the rest of the country was a wasteland of rednecks and fools, living in squalor and poverty. Luckily, parts of the towpath were so secluded you could almost believe you were in the country, but only a few miles from the fizz and crackle of the city.

In the early evening, before going to the pub, his father would practice his instruments, his bass guitar, acoustic guitar, electric guitar, his mandolin, even his old banjo. He said he felt they were looking at him reproachfully, yearning to be played. He devoted time to them all.

As Dad played cross-legged on the floor, humming to himself and swigging beer, a roll-up fixed between his stained fingers, the hard pads of flesh on his right hand, where he held down the notes, flying across the frets, Gabriel had worked too. He drew his father's face and hands; he drew the guitars and the faces of his school friends; he experimented with crayons, with pen and ink, and paints: he and his father together, both lost in something.

It was dark when they arrived now at Dad's new place. Gabriel had the impression that his father wanted to get there as late as possible. It was a vast collapsing house sliced into dozens of small rooms.

"Magnificent old building, full of original features," said Dad. "Worth millions. My room is the penthouse, at the top."

Gabriel took a camera from his rucksack. "You stand over there, Dad, by that rotting pillar."

"Later. Put it away."

"Dad—"

"Put it away, I said. You might notice . . . there are some strange characters here. You'd learn a lot if you talked to them. It's a bit like the sixties."

"Cool."

"Right."

His father spoke of the sixties with reverence, in the way others spoke of "the war": as a time of great deeds and unrepeatable excitement. Somehow, all the windows everywhere were open, and, in a "universal moment," God's favorite album, *Sgt. Pepper's,* was being played for the first time. Many of Dad's sentences would begin: "One day in the sixties . . ." as in "One day in the sixties when I was playing Scrabble with Keith Richards—he was a particularly tenacious opponent and fond of the word 'risible' . . ."

Gabriel thought he might make a film about his father entitled *One Day in the Sixties.* Gabriel suspected that his father had actually been quite young in the "sixties," and that he'd seen less of it than he liked to make out. But fathers didn't like to be doubted; fathers lacked humor when it came to themselves.

In the hallway Dad said, "Now, deep breath, heads down. There isn't a lift, I'm pleased to say. This is an opportunity for much-needed exercise."

Gabriel kept his head down but couldn't help noticing that the colorless stair carpet was ripped and stained. When he looked up he saw that on each landing there were toilets and waterlogged showers. Outside the rooms, bearded men in robes, turbans, fezzes and tarbooshes seemed to talk backwards in undiscovered languages.

Dad followed Gabriel awkwardly, stopping to rest at each bend. He had a limp, or "war wound," which sometimes he told strangers he had acquired in the "revolutionary struggle of making the world a better place, with free food and marijuana all round." In fact his "wound" was of an altogether more ignoble, though—to some—more amusing, origin.

When at last they got to the top, and Dad had to stop and lean against a damp peeling wall for a breather, which left a white mark on his coat, Gabriel took his father's key and inserted it into the lock. But the lock was stuck and the door already open. Gabriel reached out and snapped on the overhead light.

"A cosy little place." Dad's breath seemed to scrape in his throat. "It could be pretty fine, eh? What d'you think?"

Gabriel looked about.

Dad was not unclean but he was the sort who'd wipe a room over in July and be surprised in December that the grime had returned. Not that there was much anyone could do with this room.

The wind seethed at the rattling window, like an animal trying to get in; the basin in the corner was sprinkled with cigarette ash. There was a single bed covered by an eiderdown and blanket.

Gabriel couldn't help wondering what Archie would have thought.

"Original features, eh? What's in the other room?"

"What other room?" said his father. "The English never stop talking about property. The price of their house is the price of their life. They'd trade their souls for a sofa. Have you ever known me to cling to material possessions? I'm asking you, Gabriel, how many rooms does a man need?"

"Well, one for sitting in and one for—"

"Don't get technical with me, boy. This is the best I could get . . . for the money I have."

"Have your mates been here?"

"No. No one. I couldn't exactly have a supper party. I've been writing letters, though. I didn't think, when I was younger, that I would end up here. It's not that I'm particularly foolish. I can't even explain to myself how such things happen."

"That's all right, Dad."

"It's very disturbing, the sudden feeling that your life is already over, that it's too late for all the good things you imagined would happen."

"Dad, it's not."

"No. I've been trying to see this break as a beginning but this room keeps making me think that I've been here before."

"Déjà vu or reincarnation?" said Gabriel. "Are you beginning to believe in weird—?"

"What? No. Stop it. This is what everywhere looked like when I was a kid, before the world bent a bit—"

"In the sixties?"

"That's right," said Dad.

"Cool."

Presumably, his father's clothes were in the wardrobe. As for music, Dad had brought a few tapes and only one acoustic guitar, leaving his other instruments with a friend, for fear they would be stolen from the room.

"What do you do here?"

"What does anyone do anywhere? You know me: if I need a song I'll sing one. Now, I should feed you otherwise your mother will accuse me of . . . unspeakableness. Was she nervous of letting you come here?"

Gabriel didn't want to tell his father what Mum had said the previous night, when she woke him up to talk about the next day. Dad hadn't "disciplined" Gabriel sufficiently; Gabriel was doing badly at school because of his father's bad example. Hannah had been brought in to aid the "discipline" process. If it showed signs of breaking down, further "measures" would be taken; and if, during Gabriel's visit, Dad started drinking, "you're to call me," she said, "and I'll fetch you home. If he depresses you, or it's too squalid, ring and I'll be there."

Gabriel said, "Not really, Dad. I think she wants to do other things now."

"Like what?"

"I'm not really sure. Just something else."

"Right, well, that's exactly what I want to do, too. Let's eat, pal."

On the single gas burner, Gabriel had noticed an opened tin

of ravioli, black around the bottom and with a spoon in it, probably still hot.

"Wait," Gabriel said.

From his bag he produced some tacks and pinned the picture of the yellow chair over his father's bed.

He regretted it was a copy of another picture; he wished he had done something original. He would do something original.

In the meantime the yellow chair would do.

It reminded him that he had been intending to speak to Dad about the "hallucinations" and other strange scenes and nightmares taking place within the theater of his mind. He saw now that his father was burdened enough as it was.

Gabriel finished pinning the picture up and noticed his father's eyes were as wet as the wall.

"Magic," said Dad. "A few more of those and I'll be tickling myself under the chin rather than trying to cut my throat. You're good to me, Angel. I hope, whatever happens, that I will be the same to you. I think we should find a restaurant."

"Cool."

"Stop saying that!"

In the pizza place Dad ate nothing but drank a beer and watched Gabriel, asking him about school and his friends. Gabriel didn't know if his father had lost his appetite; it occurred to him that Dad couldn't afford to eat.

He said, "Where have you been, Dad?"

"Yes, sorry. Trying to get my life started again—"

"Why didn't you phone? I thought you'd gone gay."

"Gay?" Dad looked shocked. Then he laughed. "I remember you said that's what happened to your friend Zak's father. One day he woke up and decided he wanted to be with boys. Why would that happen to me? Didn't Zak's father always collect teapots? And you say he didn't know he was homosexual! Have I ever taken such a turn with teapots or any such fancy, nancy objects?"

Gabriel recalled Zak's father, who had had blond streaks painted into his thinning hair and wore tight white T-shirts with a packet of Marlboros shoved up the sleeve.

Zak and Gabriel had been friends since the first day at school, when they discovered that they not only liked the same films and music but were likely to have the same enemies.

Zak's parents were well off; his father was a computer magazine publisher and his mother a journalist. Zak had been sent to a state school rather than a fee-paying one "on principle." While he might not be the recipient of any worthwhile information at the school, at least, it was thought, for the only time in his life, he would mix with ordinary people, an education almost worth paying for. Some other kids were in the same situation: their parents were politicians or actors, or they ran the local arts cinema where Gabriel and Zak were let in for free. These kids were bullied for being "snobs," as if they were slumming or thought they were doing the school a favor by attending it, popping in for a lesson after breakfasting with their parents and the children of other celebrities in some hip Notting Hill café where models, producers and movie stars took their first calls of the day. The rough kids knew that no parents in their right mind—unless they were spectacularly privileged or politically perverse—would actually volunteer to send their child to the school.

Zak had never been poor. He didn't know what it was like. The established middle class had different fears from everyone else. They would never be desperate for money; they would never go down for good.

Sometimes Gabriel was regarded in the same light as Zak. Although there was no question of his parents being able to send him anywhere else and Gabriel's father turned up at the school not in a car, like some other parents, but on his bicycle, waiting outside with a roll-up and a newspaper he had pulled from a dustbin, he was still regarded as a "rock star" for having played with the still popular Lester Jones. He was both derided and admired for this. The kids would sing Lester's songs in the playground behind Gabriel's back.

Gabriel said now, "You used to wear glitter and makeup."

"Of course I did! I was a pop boy. Heterosexual Englishmen love getting into a dress. It's called pantomime. Anyhow, I admire Zak's dad."

"You do?"

"Changing his whole life like that. It's a big, magnificent thing to do. Funny how everyone seems to be living a bohemian life now, except for people in the government, who have to be saints. And me." He said grandly, "I have had a job."

"A job?" said Gabriel.

"Your surprise surprises me. I've been in gainful employment—out in the fresh air."

"What for?"

"It was just a fantasy I had. Gabriel, I was a sort of coolie. A bicycle courier."

"What happened?"

"I found it very hard, very hard. I got sick. It exhausted me. The distances, across London, were too great for me. I had no idea this city was so . . . undulating."

"What's that mean?"

"Fucking hilly. I thought my chest would explode."

"You've stopped doing it?"

"I . . . sort of collapsed. I'm looking for something more brain-based."

"Like what?"

"Don't ask so many questions. How's the film?"

"It's nearly ready to be shot," lied Gabriel. "All I've got to do now is save up for a movie camera."

"I wish I could help you. I will get you a camera from somewhere, I promise. What we need is a stroke—one stroke of luck. Tell me what else has been happening at home."

"We've got a hairy au pair called Hannah."

"I know. I saw her watching me. What was her last job, turning on the gas in Auschwitz?"

"Actually, she's an immigrant. She's lost in a bad dream. Most of the time she doesn't know where she is."

"Yes, yes, sorry. And this woman is lazing around in those leather chairs I got for a good price? I hope she hasn't scratched them up."

"Not at all. Mum exchanged them for a new futon."

"She exchanged them! Didn't you try to stop her?"

"You know what she's like when she makes up her mind. Out they went!" Dad looked away. Gabriel said, "Now she's at work, waitressing. You know that, too."

"Has anyone come round?"

"Sorry?"

"To the house."

"Only Mum's friends—Norma, that fat woman who always says, 'Kiss me, stupid.' And the other women—Angie and that lot—who wear big overcoats and too many scarves."

"Anyone I don't know? Strangers?"

Gabriel shook his head. "No, no strangers."

Dad drank his beer. "I'm afraid she's going to find it tough to survive without me there to guide her. When she phones for advice, I might refuse her. You will learn that women like to think they get by without us. But we give them—"

"What?"

"Erm . . . stability."

Gabriel pushed his plate away. "Don't want any more."

Dad finished the pizza himself, wiping his mouth with his sleeve.

"Why are you looking at me like that?" said Gabriel.

"Apart from your hair, you look so much like your mother. You sound like her, too."

"I can't help it, Dad."

"No, no, course not. Come on."

Back at the room Gabriel sat on the edge of the bed. Looking at his father's acoustic guitar he had the feeling Dad hadn't touched it for a while. "Dad, will you play?"

"I don't think so. I think a game of noughts and crosses will cheer us up. You used to love it."

Gabriel remembered—maybe it was only a few years after Archie died—asking his father, "What are songs for?"

"Amongst other things, to make us feel better," his father had replied, "when things are so hard."

This remark made Gabriel start to believe in the uses of entertainment.

He said, "I want to draw a man playing a guitar. There's a picture here I want to copy. If you play . . . it helps me concentrate."

"Really?"

"Please."

It was Picasso's *Blind Guitarist,* which featured an emaciated, long-limbed, blue figure, not playing his guitar but resting over it sadly.

While Gabriel studied it, his father reached for his beer can and cigarette, and started to play a blues tune with his eyes closed. He even played a little bottle-neck guitar, explaining in his endearing but inevitably pompous way that the song was one of the oldest of modern music.

"You have to settle in a very deep part of yourself when you play the blues."

"Right. I see."

Gabriel opened his sketchbook and started to draw. Sometimes when he copied something he altered the original picture; this time he cheered up the blue guitarist, giving him sight and pleasure in what he was doing.

There was a loud banging on the wall.

"Turn it off!" shouted someone.

"Who's that?" asked Gabriel.

"Turn it off!"

"They're madmen," said Dad. "The room next door. Unusual place, full of mad characters."

"We're praying!"

Gabriel said, "From the sixties?"

"Whenever," said his father. "They're not going to last into the next century." He shouted, "Pray on, mothers!"

Dad's face was starting to churn. When the banging happened again Gabriel became apprehensive. At home his father had thrown plates, books and records around, though nothing too valuable; he could sulk for days, or walk around the streets in a fury for hours. He could take five steps up the road and find someone to argue with. Had he been a woman, he might have been called hysterical. Instead, he was deemed "moody," which, because of its "artistic" overtones, unfortunately suited him. Whenever it was said, he turned up his collar and looked for a mirror, a move Gabriel liked to imitate for his mother's benefit, saying, "The James Dean of Hammersmith." It always amused her.

Yet his father had, with Gabriel, almost always been his best self. Gabriel was the one thing he'd been consistently proud of.

Dad threw his guitar down, removed his shoe, and smashed at the wall with it.

"Leave us alone!" he yelled, hopping up and down. "If you want to discuss it, meet me in the corridor, motherfucker!"

"Go to hell!" the neighbor called.

"And you, and you! See me outside!"

Gabriel tried to distract his father.

"Look at what I've done!"

He was holding up his sketchbook.

His father sat with his head in his hands. At last he studied the picture and smiled.

"Beautiful. You're getting better and better. Let's get out of this dump."

"Where?"

"Maybe we should watch TV, eh? A couple of hours of stupidity might calm us down. My nerves are twanging like piano wires."

"I wish I'd brought some videos."

For years they'd watched films together. *The Graduate* was one of their favorites, with a soundtrack they liked. *Performance,* too—kept in a plain cover—Gabriel was allowed to watch, when Mum wasn't around. *The Godfather* they had seen repeatedly, and most of Woody Allen, particularly *Play It Again, Sam. Summer with Monika, My Life as a Dog* and anything by Laurel and Hardy, as well as Tarkovsky, they knew backwards. Gabriel could repeat the dialogue as it played and used to run the films, with the sound down, as he did his homework. If each frame of a film told a story, he had to watch them repeatedly, until he knew them. Then he started to imagine the scene with his own characters in them, speaking his dialogue.

Gabriel glanced around the room, wondering whether the TV and video were concealed in a cupboard.

"Where is the telly?"

"Downstairs. There's no TV in this room. That would be an extra. Extras are out. Extras are well out."

In a smoke-filled room on the ground floor, they watched a program about a garden makeover, joining a handful of preoccupied foreign men staring up at the television, which was padlocked to an iron arm extending from the wall.

It wasn't long before Gabriel's neck began to ache from looking up.

"Boring," Gabriel was about to say, when he noticed that his father wasn't even looking at the screen but, like the other men, seemed to have become uncontactable.

A man wearing a long white robe and slippers that curled at the end like question marks came to the door.

"Phone."

"Dad." Gabriel nudged his father, who looked blankly at the hooded-eyed man.

"Phone," the man repeated.

"Who is it?" Dad turned to Gabriel, "Not that I know anyone!"

"Maybe it's Mum," said Gabriel.

"What would she want? To check up on you? You're all right here, aren't you? Haven't I been looking after you?"

"Yes," said Gabriel.

The man said, "Lester."

Dad stood up. "Lester? Did you say Lester?"

"Yes. I think I did say that name several times."

Dad gripped Gabriel's arm.

"Gabriel boy, it's Lester—Lester Jones on the phone to us—right now!"

Gabriel followed his father to the door and watched him flapping up the hall. His "war wound," which, oddly enough, he had actually acquired when with Lester, had miraculously mended.

From the door, Gabriel scrutinized his father talking animatedly to Lester. He noticed that the man who had called Dad to the phone had not gone away but was also watching his father, from the other end of the hall.

Dad finished talking and replaced the receiver.

"Gabriel—" he began.

The man in the curly slippers went to Dad, grabbed him by the shoulders, pushed him against the wall and wagged his finger at him. As the man addressed him, Dad struggled and knocked his ear. When someone else went past, the man let him go.

For a moment they stood there, snarling at one another. Gabriel was about to attack the man with his fists and feet; Dad ordered him to stay where he was.

"Don't mention any of this to Mum." White-faced and shaking, Dad was pushing Gabriel away. "It'll only make her worry. Promise?"

"OK. But what did he want?"

"Forget it! Listen: we've been stroked. I knew we would be. It was Lester on the phone! Lester—speaking to me!"

If Dad was mellow, he would talk of the time he had toured the world, playing bass for Lester Jones in the Leather Pigs, more than twenty-five years ago.

He would open a shoe box full of photographs and pictures cut from magazines and newspapers of him and Lester together. At that time Lester was one of the world's biggest pop stars, idolized and followed by millions of fans in dozens of countries, his songs and style imitated by many other groups. Like most pop heroes, Lester contained the essential ingredients of both tenderness and violence, and was neither completely boy nor girl, changing continuously as he expressed and lost himself in various disguises.

In this world before Gabriel was born, people did stranger things than they seemed to now. It amused Dad to boast of "going to bed in Memphis and waking up in San Francisco." He had worn a silver suit open at the front to reveal a shaggy chest on which a heavy medallion bounced. He had padded shoulders on which his curly hair rested—so luxuriant that Gabriel wondered where he had obtained the wig—and dark eye shadow, applied only "approximately," as well as what looked like his grandmother's earrings. On his feet, fatefully, Dad wore boots with platform soles.

Mum, who had just left art school, helped with the costumes. That was how she and Dad had met, she on her knees, measuring Dad's inside leg for a pair of red satin trousers though he'd only requested a spangled waistcoat.

It was the platform soles, those Eiffel Towers of footwear with flashing lights in the heel, that had proved calamitous. Lester and the Leather Pigs were playing a gig in the north of Finland. It was dark on stage, and Rex, becoming overexcited as a woman in the audience bared her chest, essayed an ill-advised shimmy. Normally, when performing, he didn't stir at all; Lester did more than enough of that for the whole band.

Suddenly Rex twisted his ankle. As he struggled to maintain his balance, he saw Lester smiling at him, imagining that Rex was dancing. Rex crashed down from his platform boots to find himself grovelling on the floor of the stage like an injured insect. Craggy roadies immediately ran to him. But instead of rushing him to the hospital, they attempted to reinstate Rex so that he could complete the gig, propped up like a shattered ornament between a couple of speakers.

It was discovered that Rex's leg and ankle were broken. The roadies suggested that for the rest of the tour Rex be held up in a harness, suspended from the ceiling, not unlike a puppet. Rex objected to this humiliation; while the band completed the tour, he made his way home.

By the time Rex had mended, Lester had moved on to a style of music involving flatter shoes, funkier tunes and darker hair. When Rex begged Lester to let him rejoin him Lester insisted he wanted a different sound and less hirsute musicians. Rex volunteered to shave his body, but he never worked with Lester again.

Dad had first gone to gigs as a teenager. It wasn't long before he was playing live himself. He loved the fear and anticipation of walking on stage with a band, and the noise of the crowd and their adoration. He liked seeing different cities and concert halls. He began to understand the need of actors to perform; he knew, too, that they never did the same thing every night. He believed the audience understood that what he was playing was different, or difficult, or ironic, or was just what was required in the circumstances.

After a good gig there were parties and backstage foolishness. Dad said that then you were your own drug, and the intoxication lasted several hours, though it wasn't long before you had to repeat it. It was a "sailor's" existence that Dad thought would be his life, insulated from the steep complications of the everyday world, like having to prepare food or form relationships that could survive daylight.

Following the accident he did, after a year, go on the road with Charlie Hero, a follower of Lester Jones whose music resembled Jones's. But Dad was getting older. In the bands he played with, though he was often the most accomplished musician, he was made to stand at the side of the stage, in shadow, where he got cold and had to wear thick socks; he was kept out of the videos for being too ugly, and eventually out of the bands altogether.

Before the accident Dad had been known as Free-standing Fred. Unlike many musicians, he rarely drank or used stimulants. But after it he was known as Restless Rex. People said he could never stand unaided again, without a drink in his hand.

After the phone call from Lester, Dad bought some beers to celebrate. They hurried up the stairs once more and lay down together in the single bed.

"I like a hard bed," said Dad.

"Good for our backs."

"Exactly."

"Dad, your ear is bleeding." Gabriel fetched a wet towel and bathed his father's ear. "Now keep still."

"That really was Lester Jones. He's been receiving my correspondence."

"You write to him?"

"Always have. His manager and I once spent a night in jail together. I keep Lester informed about what's going on in the real world and so on."

"How would you know?"

"Don't be cheeky."

"I didn't know you were writing to him."

"There's a lot you don't know about me. I go to cafés with the other old men, and just write anything. Children only see a small part of their parents."

"Oh," said Gabriel. "Will I be shocked by you? Should I see a psychiatrist?"

"I've witnessed it, pal. When the parents go mad, they rush their kids onto the couch. Isn't that what happened to Zak?"

"Yeah, when his old man came out—over Sunday lunch—Zak was sent to a suit who asked him dirty questions and told him to express himself."

"Did he express himself?"

"So much so that his mother stopped him going and told the psychiatrist to see a psychiatrist. She had thought it would make Zak good, not rebellious."

Dad was laughing.

"Luckily for you, we can't afford that funny stuff. And you're a beautiful kid, Angel." He went on, "Lester's been commissioned to work on his autobiography. The only problem is, his head is riddled with holes. All I've lost is my hair. Lester needs to be reminded of what close mates we were, and how I helped him make those records. That's partly my guitar sound on there. It was me who told him to be bold. 'Go further,' I said all the time. 'Be as mad as you can be.' He always reminded me of Orson Welles."

"Sorry? Is that the younger Welles or the older? When are you going to see him?"

"When are *we* going, you mean?"

"You're taking *me?*"

"Tomorrow morning."

"I'm supposed to be at school."

Dad hesitated. "You've had more than enough education. Lester is more important than algebra. Promise you won't tell Mum." Dad started to roll a joint. "Don't tell her anything about me, except that there's some kicking life in your old dad yet."

Two years ago the three of them had gone to see Lester perform in a football stadium. He, Mum and Dad spent the day searching through boxes in order to dress up in "Lester" gear, seventies clothes, glitter and makeup, applied by Mum. Of course, Lester walked on stage wearing a dark suit, although he did wear high heels with it. Gabriel had been pained to see his father among the ticket touts and pushing hysterical crowd, ankle-deep in the rubbish on the floor, surrounded by people wearing T-shirts with Lester's face on, knowing Dad could have been rocking on stage.

"Dad, can you tell me who that man was?" said Gabriel.

"Which man?"

"The one who held you against the wall. What does he want?"

"Don't ask. He wants . . . only money. He was good enough to lend me something a few days ago, when I was cycling for the company. I thought I'd be able to pay him back."

"And will you?"

"I think we'll be all right now."

"How?"

"Lester will take care of us. I'm certain of it. I'll be out of here in a few weeks. Maybe in a few days. It's going to be the high life for us! I'm thinking of taking you to New York for a bit."

"New York!"

"We're going into the pleasure zone! Now, let's get into this bed."

Gabriel and his father undressed to their underwear and got into the tiny bed. As a child Gabriel had loved sleeping wedged between his parents; they had had to repeatedly replace him in his own cold bed. Now he wished he had his own bed, for with a burp, fart and a tug, his father pulled the eiderdown over himself, not realizing Gabriel was left with only a thin sheet to cover him.

His father was excited, wondering aloud whether Lester might give him a job in the new band he was taking on the road;

or perhaps he might want to hear one of Dad's recent songs, or even write one with him. He became dreamy, Dad, when he'd had a smoke.

Dad then started to imagine the kind of flat—in a mansion block, with a porter—he would buy with the money from this enterprise.

"What I want, one day," said his father, "is for you and me to live together again."

"You mean you're thinking of coming home?"

"Why? Does Mum keep saying she wants me to?"

"Not exactly."

"Right. What I do want is my own place and to come home from a gig somewhere, knowing you're there sometimes, my son. I can't wait for that."

Gabriel tried to encourage his father away from these speculations by bringing the subject round to music.

Dad was soon "monologuing" about the Beatles, Jimi Hendrix and the Doors; about soul music, and Aretha Franklin, Nina Simone and the Supremes. He talked of how the lyrics and the music worked together and of the work's cultural and political context.

When at last his father fell asleep, still muttering about why the brass on one record was better than on another, Gabriel was able to relax at last. He thought about painting, and about Degas, and then Degas's girls. He couldn't sleep with an erection. He masturbated quickly—taking care not to splash his father—and slipped from the bed.

He heard doors slamming in the depths of the house; someone laughed for a long time; he thought he heard a window break and a rat scratching behind the skirting board; he saw, under the newspaper, the corner of a crumpled pornographic magazine and read the words "beyond blue." He thought of two boys whose mothers were dead, Lennon and McCartney, in Paul's front room, writing songs all afternoon, with guitars in their laps, wanting to be the best. He whispered to Archie, but even he didn't respond.

All sleeping; all safe. But not Gabriel, not tonight, with so much to think about.

He opened the window, finished Dad's joint and threw it down to the street, watching the little sparks scatter and expire in the darkness.

Sitting on the windowsill, next to Dad's milk and trainers, and looking out over West London, he took out his sketchbook and pencils and drew his sleeping, open-mouthed father, with little snores, like bubbles, emerging from his mouth into the cold room. Meanwhile, in this city, not far away, Lester Jones was living and breathing, with Rex on his mind. Tomorrow he would see them both.

Three

Gabriel awoke alone, pulled aside the filthy net curtains and rubbed a clear space in the window. The weather was bright and clear.

He guessed that Dad had risen early to wash and shave before the queues started outside the bathrooms. The door opened and Dad came into the room with tea and cold toast, which Gabriel ate quickly, sitting on the bed.

Gabriel had almost forgotten the numerous labored groans, coughs, splutterings and self-aimed muttered criticisms it took to get his father started in the morning. Then Gabriel packed his things while Dad snipped at his sideburns with blunt scissors in a cloudy mirror. Gabriel noticed that his father's hands were trembling. Dad's euphoria of the previous night had been replaced by anxiety—he kept pulling at his nose and ears and sticking his tongue out like a lizard.

Staring in the mirror he said suddenly, "Look, I've got acne too. Here, under my nose, a crop of it. I've almost retired and I've got more acne than you."

Dad was making Gabriel tense. "It's like we're going to visit a King or Prince," he said.

"Yes, except that Lester has achieved his position because of his own work, rather than everyone else's. To think, that a person could live like him."

"What d'you mean?"

"As a free man. He can buy a house in any city in the world. He can look at glaciers and deserts whenever he wants. He can meet any person. Scientists, musicians and psychologists will run to him if he asks. And why is that?"

"Why is it?"

Ponderously Dad explained that Lester had the one thing that everyone wanted, something rarer than rubies or even the ability to make money, the force at the center of the world which made precious and important things happen. This was his imagination or talent. This was his gift.

No one knew, even now, how such abilities or power originated or worked. Like love it couldn't be forced, bottled, transferred or analyzed. Certainly, anyone who could figure out how to make or grow it would be more rewarded than anyone in history. How could Dad and Gabriel not be intimidated?

"What's wrong, Dad?"

Dad was looking Gabriel over.

"Tuck your shirt in. Couldn't you have brought some better clothes?"

"I was only coming to see you."

Dad pulled at Gabriel's hair. "Haven't you even combed this?"

"I never touch it, you know that. I'm superstitious!"

"Comb it!" said Dad. Gabriel shoved his father's comb into the matted blond mess and looked up. Dad said, "But it doesn't look any different!"

"You put that joint down," said Gabriel. "What would Mum say? She's always warning me against that sort of thing."

"You're right," said Dad, hiding it behind his back. "I think we'd better go."

They retrieved Dad's bicycle from where it was chained to nearby railings and Gabriel clambered onto the crossbar, his bag on his back. He had always ridden on Dad's bicycle, or followed on his own.

"Straight on 'til morning," announced Gabriel, as he liked to when the two of them set off together.

"Prepare to lose your mustache!" Dad replied.

Gabriel was heavy now and Dad had to stand on the pedals with his head up, like someone trying to look into the far distance. Gabriel thought they might have progressed more rapidly had they reversed their positions, but it wasn't a good time to risk discouraging his father.

They heaved through the traffic until they came to a less ragged part of town where the cars were quicker, the buildings more curvaceous, and the people dressed in clothes that fitted, with modern haircuts and expensive bodies.

Dad secured the bike to a lamppost at the end of the street. Then they walked, or "legged it," as Dad put it. Dad didn't want to be seen arriving at Lester's on a knackered bicycle, though Gabriel wondered who exactly his father imagined might see them. He didn't think Lester would be standing on the street outside his hotel.

"This is the place." Dad's face changed to wonder. "Look. There. I told you."

Gabriel followed his father's glance up the road. There was a crowd on the pavement outside what he presumed was Lester's hotel.

"Come," said his father. "Let's get started."

Gabriel noticed, as they got closer, that the throng was composed of many men and women of different ages wearing the clothes Lester had sported more than twenty years before, as if God the cartoonist had had Lester followed, for life, by mocking imitations in order to constrain his pride.

Less strange but more threatening were the score or so of photographers with bands of equipment strapped to them, some of them standing on boxes to get a sterling view of what looked like a brick wall.

Although Dad was as surprised by all this as Gabriel, it pleased him, too.

"This was what it was like in the old days, boy." They were approaching. "Everywhere we went, crowds of people waving and shouting and wanting to touch us."

"Even you?"

"Even me, I'm afraid, you bloody idiot. I was successful too young. At twenty-five I had everything a kid could use, and a lot a kid couldn't."

Gabriel and his father hesitated at the edge of the crowd. The photographers turned and stared at Gabriel's father, Nikons and Canons raised, lenses protruding.

"Excuse me," said Dad.

No one moved. There was a puzzled pause.

"Is he anyone?" a voice asked.

"Is he? Is he?" said other people.

"No, no one," was the authoritative reply, at last.

"No one," someone echoed.

"No, no one."

A sigh of disappointment fluttered through the gathering.

"We are someone." Dad put his hand on Gabriel's arm. He whispered, "If anyone asks us anything . . . say 'No comment.' Right?"

"No comment," repeated Gabriel.

"That's it. And when we actually see him . . . Lester—"

"Yes?"

"Don't say too much."

"Don't talk?"

"Well, a bit." Dad's skin was bubbling with sweat like the walls of his room. "Oh God," he moaned. "It's been a long, long time!"

"Is this the hotel?"

Gabriel saw only a long, dark, high wall with a green door set into it. The brass knocker was in the shape of a monkey's head.

"Of course it is."

They passed through the crowd. Gabriel noticed that the fans had Lester's face, slightly remodeled, as if Lester had bequeathed them his old faces, having no more use for them.

"No comment," Dad intoned.

"No comment," Gabriel murmured.

No one had asked them a question.

The door opened, a man in grey holding it for them.

"Harold Steptoe?" said Dad.

"Harold is waiting," said the man.

Dad whispered to Gabriel, "That's the name Lester always uses in hotels."

They were taken across the threshold and the door closed behind them.

Gabriel, with his father beside him, found himself standing in an almost empty space.

There was a deep hush in the hotel; the place was so stylish that there appeared to be nothing to disfigure the exquisite austerity of nothing piled on nothing, apart from—on an invisible shelf—a white vase containing a single white flower.

In the distance, little figures in charcoal pajamas and slippers started to unbend slowly, like Chinese mandarins coming out of hypnosis.

One of these, a young girl, began to move towards them.

"Lester is waiting for you," she said, arriving pale, slightly out of breath and older than when she had started out. "This way."

As they followed, Gabriel thought how easy it would be to

disappear into such an expanse of nullity until he realized she made her way by following a line of little grey pebbles on the ground. Approaching a plain white wall, she turned left suddenly and went through an arch, treading along a corridor where occasionally they saw bodyguards in black, protecting Lester from madmen who wanted him to be a god.

The girl rapped on a door and was gone.

Lester opened it himself, wearing a green silk kimono.

He and Rex embraced.

"How's the ankle?" Lester took them into the room. He turned to Gabriel. "Did Rex tell you how it happened?"

"Many times."

Dad started to hop up and down on one leg. "All mended! Strong as a giraffe! Look! I'm ready to tour again!"

Gabriel took Dad's hand to calm him.

"Good," said Lester. "I'm not!"

His face was as sharp and bright as a blade; he had one brown eye and one blue, with yellow flashes across it.

Gabriel saw, in another room, a young, bare-legged woman sitting at a mirror having her hair caressed by two men in orange sarongs, their mouths filled with clips.

Lester directed Dad to a table in the corner.

"Let me pick your long-living brain, maestro," he said. "I'm trying to do some kind of memoir. The freaks I've had in here from the past, doing my remembering for me! Now . . ."

They talked over old times and Lester made notes. Gabriel took out his sketchbook and continued to work on the picture of his father he had started the previous night.

He kept looking at Lester, secretly and not so secretly.

How could he write songs that people the world over knew the words to? Why did people continue to buy his records? Why, when he played live, did people queue through the night to see him? How did people acquire such powers? Was it in Lester's hair, which was certainly magnificent and dyed ruby red? Or was the magic located in his white, long thin fingers with their round, clean nails?

Meanwhile Lester listened to Dad's reminiscences, leaning forward at first, and then further and further backwards. Dad had started out on a story about a night in a Northern town that involved someone vomiting in their own suitcase. Lester, who seemed to be erupting inwardly himself, was looking for inspiration.

"Hey! Hey!" he said suddenly. "Listen Rex. You know, I've just finished a new record. I think it's my best one in years."

"I know all your stuff. Can't wait to hear this one," said Dad.

"Do you want to hear it right now?"

Dad looked confused. "Not before you're ready. Anyway," he continued. "Plucky, Twang the guitarist and I had just checked into this bed-and-breakfast and a big consignment of supernova grass had been delivered—"

Lester said, "I've never been readier. I've got a tape of it—right here!" He popped the tape into a small machine on the table. "There's no track list." He grabbed a piece of paper. "I know what: I'll write down the song title and you jot your thoughts down underneath."

"Great idea."

Dad was starting to get annoyed but what could he do?

Lester left Dad sitting beside the tape sucking the end of a pencil, and made his way across to Gabriel. This was not straightforward, as the floor was almost concealed by different-sized sheets of paper covered with scribbles, drawings, doodles, and poems in many colors.

Gabriel remembered, from talking to his father, that Lester had been a painter before he'd been a pop star, and had continued to paint and exhibit.

"Tables aren't big enough for me," said Lester. "I prefer floors, where I can get to things." Gabriel felt Lester's different-colored eyes on him. "What were you going to say?"

Gabriel blushed. "I'm thinking that it reminds me of a kid's bedroom."

He expected Lester to be offended. Across the room, Gabriel saw his father's face twist in embarrassment and fear.

Lester laughed. "Yes, I was brought up to be neat, but I was able to teach myself to be messy and disorganized, noisy and loud. It took some learning! Good boys achieve nothing! This is what I do for a living—cover bits of paper. Look, look!" Lester got onto his knees and indicated a sheet of paper. "I found these new crayons. This is what I was doing last night."

Gabriel said, "But that's what I do."

"What do you mean?"

Gabriel jumped up and fetched his sketchbook from where he had put it down. "See."

Lester looked at the picture. "What else do you have there?"

Gabriel handed him the book. Lester went through it, page by page.

Gabriel explained, "Like you, I've been writing on the pictures. Some of them are photographs." He showed a page to Lester. "I drew these daffodils for Dad and put them next to the photographs. Then I wrote daffodil poems across them in different colors so that Dad would know what I meant. It all went together in my mind—"

"You put it all together in the picture."

"Yes."

Lester went on, "I write songs but I don't know how. When something occurs to me, I write it down and put it in the song. What does an imagination do but see what isn't there?"

"I get that a lot," said Gabriel. "Sometimes I think I'm going mad with all the stuff that's going on."

"Oh everyone's mad. But some people can do interesting things with their madness." Lester was looking at Gabriel. "You're talented," he told him. "I'm telling you—and now you know for ever. Hear my voice and carry these words wherever you go."

"I don't know. I just sit down every day and start."

"That's how to do it. Talent might be a gift but it still has to be cultivated. The imagination is like a fire or furnace; it has to be stoked, fed and attended to. One thing sets another ablaze. Keep it going."

"The thing is," said Gabriel, blushing, "I've been copying other artists. I don't know why . . . it inspires me, I suppose. Is that wrong?"

"It's what you make of the stolen objects that's important. If you take something and use it, then it's worthwhile. If you just copy it and it stays the same, then nothing's been done."

Gabriel felt excited. "How do you start?"

"Like this."

Lester took a crayon and made a line on the paper, followed by another line. He wrote a word; more words followed.

"You can't will a dream or an erection. But you can get into bed," he said. "Any mad stuff that comes into my mind I put down. Wild pigs, fauns, guitars, faces . . . in dreams the maddest connections are made! If I know where I'm going, how will I get lost on the way? When I'm doing this I disappear. There's no me there. I don't know who I am. I draw and sing to get lost. If I'm not lost how can I do anything? This is how I live twice. I live in the world, and then in memory and imagination. If you listen to the greatest music like 'Strawberry Fields' or *Cosi Fan Tutte,* or read the greatest books, like *Hamlet,* you'll see how weird, almost supernatural and dreamlike they are."

Lester kept writing, coloring in and sketching, his white hand disappearing into the white page.

"You work quickly."

"As quickly as I can, these days," said Lester, "to keep ahead of the rising tide of boredom."

With his face close to Gabriel's, Lester began to talk of himself as a young man, before he was known or successful, and the difficulty of keeping alive self-belief when there was no one to confirm it. This was the hardest time for any artist.

After a while Gabriel became aware of his father watching them from across the room. Gabriel had been so absorbed he was unaware of how much time had passed.

Dad got up as though startled from a dream.

"What did you think, Rex?" said Lester.

"What?"

"Of the new tunes? I've been working on them for a long time. I wanted them to be really good. They're an advance, aren't they? The same as before, but different enough, don't you think? I'm sick of people saying it's not up to what I did when I was twenty-five. Tell me."

Gabriel was surprised to see how apprehensive Lester was, as if it were his first record.

Dad seemed to shake himself. "As good as anything you've done. If not better. What sounds! Yes!"

"Thanks." Lester took the piece of paper, looked at it, and turned it over. "You didn't write anything down."

"No, no. I was too stunned."

"By which track in particular?"

"All of them . . . all stunned me."

"The third track—the one featuring the trumpet, and later that jumbled piano—is my favorite," said Lester. "You?"

Lester was looking at Rex.

Dad hesitated. "I liked them all. The second, the third. The fourth especially. But I think the fifth took the biscuit. I'm still writing myself. You don't want to hear one of my new songs, by any chance?"

"If only there were world enough and time."

"Of course. Anyhow, I didn't bring my guitar. I'll send you a tape to the usual place." He offered Lester his hand. "We'd better not take up any more of your time. Thanks for everything."

"That's all right, friend. I've enjoyed myself. I was going to say—I want to give you something."

"Really?" Dad smiled widely. "You don't have to. I know things will pick up after a bit. I myself am working on a bicycle—sorry, I meant cycle—of songs, on the theme of life, death and rebirth. It's a triptych. Is that how you pronounce it? But I'm sure even someone as successful as you can remember what it's like to fall on hard times . . ."

Lester interrupted: "It's for your son."

"For the boy? Good, good. What sort of thing is it?"

Lester picked up a big sheet of paper from the floor. "This."

"Oh."

"I should give it a title. What do you think, Gabriel?"

"I'm not sure."

Lester wrote "Weird Weather" on the picture, signed and dedicated it, rolled it up, slipped a rubber band around it and slotted it under Gabriel's arm.

"Put it on your wall or wherever. You might look at it now and again and remember this day. Some of the things I said might be of use. If not, it doesn't matter."

Gabriel said, "I'll remember them."

Lester touched Dad on the shoulder. "Rex, he's good, your boy. Do you spend much time with him?"

"I lost one son, a long time ago and I can't afford to lose another. So we're together a lot. I'm educating him in politics, astronomy and other stuff like that. He has always followed me around."

"Until recently," said Gabriel.

"What d'you mean?" asked Lester.

Dad's eyes darted about. "I've had to move out . . . for a bit."

"Christ, sorry to hear that. I remember Christine very well. Is that her name? I even kissed her once."

"You did?"

"Before your time, of course."

"Right."

"You won't let him down, will you?" said Lester. When he saw that Dad was taken aback, he added, "I have a daughter, you see. I hardly saw her grow up. I was away too much, working."

"No chance of that with me," said Dad.

Lester seemed to be pondering something. "Sometimes I think I became an artist because it was the only way I could avoid my parents. They argued and I escaped into the back room to read comics and draw and listen to records. Little Richard on 45— 'She's Got It'." Lester sang, "'Sweet little girl that lives down the street / I'm crazy but I say she's sweet . . . She's got it!'"

Gabriel went hot inside. Lester Jones was singing to them!

He went on, "Somehow I never stopped singing that song! And drawing! And wearing Italian jackets with white linen jeans. Not to mention the Chelsea boots and eye shadow that matched the color of the socks I was wearing!"

Lester started to laugh. Gabriel and Dad laughed along with him, like a couple of cringing courtiers, though they weren't sure what was amusing. Gabriel knew Dad would be envious of Lester's honest self-engrossment, and by the fact he could talk about himself, confident that others would listen. As a musician Dad had once been something of a little king himself; later, in his own house, at least, he had been attended to. Even that was gone.

Lester rapped on the table with his knuckle. "On we go! Forward, forward!"

The door opened and the girl in charcoal pajamas came in.

Lester waved and turned away.

Dad and Gabriel were hurried through the rinsed-out maze of the hotel.

On reaching the lobby, Gabriel extracted an apple from his pocket, which he had taken from Lester's fruit bowl. He placed it on the floor in the middle of a ring of drab stones. The little patch of color would cheer people up. He and his father passed into the crowd of photographers and fans stamping their feet in the cold. Gabriel turned to see several colorless figures scampering towards the anarchic apple.

Gabriel had wondered whether his father might be amused, too; he used to enjoy anything subversive. Once, Dad dressed up as Santa Claus and took Gabriel and his school friends into a big shop in the West End and began distributing the toys to the children. It wasn't long before Dad, Gabriel and the others were chased out by store security, who in their turn were pursued by children outraged to see a benevolent Santa arrested. Outside, they laughed until they choked.

There was no opportunity for amusement now.

Four

As they started to shoulder through the noisy crowd—and it was easier for Gabriel, being smaller—he glanced back to see that something was holding his father up.

One of Lester's fans, an old woman, had laid the white claw of her hand on Dad's arm and was pinning him to her.

"Excuse me," she was saying. "One second only, sir!"

"No comment," parroted Dad, trying to pull away.

Gabriel had to jump up and down to catch a glimpse of his father, clutching Lester's picture to him.

"Dad, Dad—come on!"

He was about to return to grab his father's hand and tug him free. The woman, searching frantically for something in her mind, suddenly said, "But—Rex! Rex!"

"Who are you?" Gabriel's father peered into her old face as if he might see other, younger ones, underneath. "I don't recognize you."

"I was there. It was me that saw . . . that saw—"

"Where were you? What did you see?"

"In Finland, where you fell from your superboots. I used to follow the group around. You were the bass player."

"I was that man!"

"A lovely smooth bass line you had, too."

"You noticed?"

"I was watching when your ankle went. I heard you cry out. Then you were down. 'Oh God, he's had it,' I thought, and I wanted to run to you and kiss you back to life and—"

Her voice was drowned out as a voice rose in the crowd: "Lester's bass player!"

"He was in the Leather Pigs!"

"It's Rex! He's alive!"

"He's returned from Iceland!"

"He's been to see Lester! He's touched him!"

"Rex! Rex!"

"Look over here Mr. Pig Rex!" cried a photographer. "Smile for your fans!"

"Smile, smile, smile!"

The crowd had turned to Gabriel's father, pushing and shoving to get a better view. Some people clambered onto the backs of others. Gabriel saw that Dad didn't know whether to be delighted or humiliated by the attention.

The woman went on, "You were the most attractive Pig. I always looked at you the most—after Lester," she added, unnecessarily.

Dad said, "D'you remember my paisley glitter suit and the silver shoes with hearts?"

"Oh yes, yes I do—Oh the silver shoes!"

"And the red satin—"

Gabriel realized that the fans were not plucking at his father, but that they wanted to touch him, as if he could cure or save them. For a moment he looked like someone wearing a costume made of hands.

The woman said, "I beg you—let me have your autograph."

Dad quickly signed her book. He bent forward and kissed her. At this the other fans started to wave their books at Dad, heaving forward in a threatening way. For a moment Dad went under the crowd.

"Run!" shouted Gabriel, when his father's bald patch bobbed up again. "Run, Dad! Run!"

Ensuring that his father was hopping and tripping behind him, Gabriel started to run himself, breaking out of the crowd and into the freedom of the ordinary street with its shoppers and office workers. Neither of them stopped until they reached the end of the road.

Dad was white and shaken; he held his chest and found it difficult to speak.

"I thought they were going to devour me and spit me out."

"Just like the old days?"

"Too much like that. Though less well paid."

"Good fun, though. Wait till people hear about it."

"Don't tell Mum."

"Why not?"

"It's not a good idea. Promise?"

His father unchained the bicycle. Gabriel looked back at the hotel.

A black car with dark windows emerged from further along the brick wall and swept towards them, the dignified whisper of its wheels suggesting that it barely touched the earth. Lester's fans and photographers spotted the car and started to hurtle along behind it, some of them falling down and getting trampled, their autograph books and pens flung from their hands. At least they no longer had any interest in Dad.

The car passed and Dad waved. "There's Lester—going to the airport."

"Where's he off to?"

"He owns an island where he is protected by barbed wire

and gunboats. He's not a fool—he has always known that fame is a handful of foam. He recognized too, that fame isn't a tap you can turn on and off at will. But it was a price he had to pay for what he wants to do. Lester can't roam the streets like us." Dad glanced up and down the street. "Not that he'd be missing much."

It wasn't fame that Lester had warned Gabriel about when they lay on the floor together. It was envy, which Lester called one of the strongest human forces: the jealousy and hatred of others, and their desire to contain or undermine you. He said the temptation in the face of such a force might be to make oneself as inconspicuous as possible, to merge, blend in, not seem more talented than other people. However, if you attempted that—trying to "disappear" yourself or live undercover—you would rob yourself of your own gifts. Lester said it was important to find people who were supportive and inspiring, and who didn't mock one's hopes.

The car accelerated into the distance and Gabriel thought of the pale, isolated figure within, writing, drawing and perhaps humming, with a kind of contentment, "She's Got It."

Dad said suddenly, "Where's the picture?"

Gabriel tapped it. "Right here, Dad. Safe."

"Good, good. I'll hold on to it, I think. I found that a very interesting meeting with Lester. Let's go to a café and have a talk."

Gabriel reminded his father, "I'm still supposed to be at school."

"I forgot about that. Do you fancy some education?"

"I've had enough of that for one day."

Dad took the picture and pushed it down the front of his coat.

They went to a café nearby where Dad wiped the damp table down with his cuff. He slipped off the rubber band and unrolled the picture. To keep it flat Gabriel placed a sauce bottle on one end, and a pot of mustard on the other.

"Not bad, not bad at all."

Dad put on his glasses and assumed a voice like an antique dealer on a television program evaluating an old object.

"I didn't get the chance to look at it properly just now," he went on. "For what it is, it's pretty interesting. I thought it might just be a sketch."

"It's not that," said Gabriel, leaning over it.

Like his father, Gabriel could see it was a complete, coherent picture, rather than a sketch or selection of scribbles. Lester had probably been working on it for a while.

"It's dedicated to you, and signed," said Dad. "Lester was very friendly, just as I predicted. He's always been like that with me."

"Did you enjoy his new album?"

"Yes, yes I did," said Dad, airily. "There can't be many people who have heard it. We were lucky to be so honored."

Meanwhile the waitress had come over and was looking at the picture.

"Did you do it?" she said to Gabriel. "It's pretty."

"It is, yes."

"I wish I could draw like that."

Glancing up at his father Gabriel wondered what exactly was wrong; he appeared to be grimacing and gurning at her.

"We're brothers." Dad pointed at Gabriel. "He's the eldest."

She bit her lip. "What can I get you?"

"What d'you think I might like?"

"I'm run off my feet," she said. "Come on."

"You come on. We're artists."

"Piss artists."

"That's funny. Say it again. Go on."

Dad wouldn't stop looking at her. Gabriel ordered hot chocolate and cheesecake for both of them.

Dad watched her go, before saying, "What we should do is this. We should see what the picture is worth."

"What do you mean—what it's worth?"

"I think we're in business. We could get a reasonable price for it."

"For this picture?"

Dad nodded.

Gabriel said, "Didn't Lester give you any money?"

"Did you want me to humiliate myself by asking? I'm a musician not a beggar. But we could do something with this." He rubbed his forehead. "To be honest, Gabriel, this separation from your mother has run me into a few problems of a financial nature."

Gabriel thought of the man who had threatened his father, pushing him against the wall so that Dad hit his head and hurt his ear. Perhaps he would do the same thing again, today.

His father said, "Years ago I was in a group with a man who now has restaurants full of rock memorabilia—gold discs, photographs, guitars, all that old tat. Young people can find interest in an old pop star's trousers. This picture is recent and it's original. I reckon he'd pay a lot for it. I'll take it to him now and see what he says."

Dad started to roll up the picture.

Gabriel said, "Right now?"

"I think it will be open. We're rocking here, boy. That's the thing about life—there are some opportunities you can't let go!"

"Listen!" Gabriel slammed his hands down on the table. "Listen, Dad."

His father looked shocked. "What's the matter, Angel?"

It was a difficult situation. Gabriel didn't know what to do. He had an idea. If he contacted his brother, Archie would—surely—supply a solution to satisfy both Gabriel and his father.

For a moment Gabriel closed his eyes but heard nothing.

Dad touched his son's face. "Gabriel, are you awake?"

"Yes. But wait—"

Perhaps Gabriel was trying too hard. After a moment he

heard the clear calm voice of his brother. Gabriel listened and nodded to himself. You could rely on Archie, sometimes.

Dad was slipping the rubber band around the picture. "Let's go. The restaurant isn't far from here."

"No, Dad."

His father looked up. "What?"

"The picture is mine."

"Yours? Of course it's yours. But haven't I given you everything? What do you think I'm trying to do here?"

"Lester gave it to *me*."

Dad rolled up his sleeves. "Look at these scratch marks! I almost got murdered carrying that picture away! That crowd wanted to rip off my clothes and eat me!"

"He didn't give it to you." This was the hardest conversation of Gabriel's life. In Archie's voice he said, "I'll keep it a few days."

"A few days!"

"I want to look at it. Let me enjoy it."

His father was looking at him in annoyance. At last he nodded and handed the picture to his son.

"You'll bring it back to me?" he said. "You can't leave such a valuable object just lying around the place. I wasn't intending to sell it, if that's what you think."

"What were you intending to do, then?"

"Get an estimate of its value, that's all."

"I'll give it back to you. I promise."

"That's pretty magnanimous of you," said Dad, sarcastically, "bearing in mind we wouldn't be in this poverty-stricken situation right now if you hadn't talked so much to Lester about your precious drawings. You forced the poor man to pretend to be interested—"

"It was Lester who did it," said Gabriel. "He was talking to me."

"You led him on. It was disgraceful, ungrateful behavior! I wish I hadn't taken you, you little idiot!"

"Calm down, Dad—"

"He hardly said two words to me. I'll be lucky if he even mentions my name in his memoirs! It was my great chance and what happened? We came away with a rotten picture you won't even let me have!"

Gabriel got up and went to the bathroom. When he returned the picture was still lying on the table. Dad wasn't in his seat.

He had backed the waitress, still holding a heavy tray, into a corner, and was talking to her while writing something on a piece of paper which he slipped into the pocket of her apron. She was looking about anxiously, as if Dad were a prickly hedge bearing down on her, and she sought a gap to dash through.

"Dad!" Gabriel called.

Dad turned; the woman scooted away.

"Oh, I'm in a better mood now," said his father. "She took my phone number! There's one thing that women like—"

"What's that?"

"They like men who want them, who have a passion for them. You remember this. See how interested she is in me."

"Are you sure she wasn't about to call the police?"

"What makes you say that? What are you saying? That I'm a dirty old fool?"

"Dad—"

"Is that it?" His father's face looked as though it had been turned inside out. Dad could flirt, but he couldn't charm. "You're right. That's me—an old man!"

"In a way."

"Does it show?"

"Now and again."

"The light is bright in here."

"Dad—"

Dad dug his fingers into his own stomach and pulled at the rolls of flesh. "You reckon I should do a few press-ups?"

"At least."

· 81 ·

"What possessed me suddenly? It was hope! Stupid hope! Gabriel . . . I've been so lonely!"

"Do you miss Mum?"

"She listened to my monologues, as she called them. All the time we were together she had at least half an ear open to me. I have so much to tell her . . . Except that she doesn't want to hear me. She got rid of my furniture!" Dad glanced back at the waitress, now secure behind the counter and looking determinedly in the other direction. "I s'pose most of us spend most of our lives trying to control our desire for other people."

Gabriel took his father's arm. "I'll see what I can do with Mum, Dad."

"Oh yes, thank you. At least we've got this," said Dad, tapping the picture.

They were leaving; the manager approached them with the bill.

"You still haven't paid, sir."

Dad looked startled and patted his thighs with both hands, as though he were playing a strange percussion. "Sorry, sorry," was the accompaniment. "These trousers don't have pockets."

Fortunately, Gabriel had some money that his mother had given him the day before.

At the end of the afternoon Dad took Gabriel home. They hadn't even reached the gate when Hannah opened the front door and stood there regarding them both.

"Hello," said Dad.

"Mr. Bunch," she said. "Day nice."

"Say something else to her, Dad. Something funny."

"What for?" said Dad.

Gabriel kissed his father's cheek. He smelled of shaving foam and himself; it was a smell Gabriel had known all his life. It reminded him of Dad taking his, Gabriel's, feet, and rubbing them against his prickly face, making Gabriel scream with laughter.

"See you, Dad."

"I hope so. I'm with you, Gabriel."

"Me, too."

Dad put his arm around Gabriel and said in a low voice, "Please don't forget—I'll be waiting in my room for the picture. Have a good look at it now, and ring me soon—tomorrow, maybe—when you've finished with it. Apart from you, it is all I have now."

It was peculiar saying goodbye to Dad outside his own house and then going in to be looked after by a woman his father didn't know, a stranger.

When Dad walked away, Gabriel saw that despite his father's efforts in the morning, his clothes looked unwashed and his hair uncut and particularly wild. His troubles looked as though they were giving him a slight stoop. Gabriel hoped he would be all right.

He would think of what he could do to help him.

Five

As soon as he got through the door of the house, Gabriel started to talk, forgetting that Hannah understood little of what he said. He wanted, at least, to show her the picture, but he doubted whether Lester's work had been carried into the distant mountains of Phlegm or its small town, Bronchitis, near Hernia.

He was tense and tired; the events of the past two days had so excited and overwhelmed him he felt he had passed through two birthdays at once without any cake.

"Where's Mum?"

"Wha?"

"Mum. The woman who lives here. Where?"

"Work," said Hannah. "To get you food to eat, lazybones."

"I forgot," said Gabriel. "Is she coming early or late?"

"Late."

He still hadn't become used to her not being there. However, he didn't want to sit around missing her. He had things to do.

Telling Hannah he had some schoolwork, he went up to Mum's room and looked for the clothes and makeup they'd worn at Lester's gig. He couldn't find the clothes, but he did find a musty old kimono, not unlike the one Lester had been wearing. It wasn't exactly winter wear, and he had to put on a T-shirt underneath, but he resembled Lester more than he had done earlier. Then he went into his own room to play Lester's records and study the picture. He drew Lester and wrote in his sketchbook all he could remember of what he had said, things like, "If I know where I'm going, how can I get lost on the way?"

He made drawings to illustrate these sayings. He knew it wasn't sufficient to worship Lester, like those fans who thought they could procure Lester's powers by copying his hair color. If Gabriel was to achieve anything himself it would take more than hair dye. He had to follow Lester's example and go his own way.

He awoke with her hair tickling his face. She had always done that when he was a baby, shaking the spray of her hair over him and laughing and making him crazy.

"How was it?" she said.

Coming to, he realized he could hear music from downstairs. Mum had brought her "friends" back to the house. Her hair smelt as if it had been dipped in cigarette smoke.

"How was what?"

He was not too sleepy to be unable to use the classic "adolescent" defense: ignorance, denial and untruth.

"You know what. Your time at Dad's place."

She sat on the edge of the bed, pulled back the covers and went to tickle him.

"Please don't do that," he said. "Mum!"

"What are you wearing?"

"Just something I found."

"You were always one for dressing up. Now tell me what happened."

He said as neutrally as he could, "I enjoyed it."

"Has he got things organized over there?"

"Not exactly organized."

"No. So—things are not good?"

"Not bad."

"What do you mean by that?"

"I don't know," parried Gabriel.

"What's Dad going to do, then?"

"You know Dad. He's got a few contacts."

Mum snorted and laughed. "With the barmen in the Nashville? There was a job in the off-licence down the road. They know him there. I thought he might as well take their money before giving it back to them. But would he do it?" She was looking at him. "Was Dad drinking?"

"Not really."

"Drugs?"

"You know I've given up."

"Him, you little fool!" She pretended to slap his face. "Don't joke about that subject."

"Sorry."

"And if he does anything like that with you around, I'll stop him seeing you."

Gabriel was listening for Archie, but he had made himself incommunicado.

After the experience of dealing with these interrogations from his parents, Gabriel wondered whether he might be qualified for work as a diplomat. Zak's parents had recently separated and Gabriel had heard about the trials of being a divorce "go-between." Generally, the code among the children, when the burning light of their parents' curiosity was turned on them, was not unlike that of criminals dealing with the police: "Say nothing; give nothing away—it'll only be used against you."

The last thing parents wanted was the truth; a child could be punished for telling it. He was learning, but the situation was relatively new to him.

He found himself saying, "That's not all Dad is. Lester was pleased to see him."

She said, "Lester who? Lester Jones?"

"He gave me a picture he'd done."

"Lester hasn't seen Dad for years. Are you making up stories? I remember when you told the teacher at school that I'd fallen into a volcano."

"Hadn't you?"

"Sort of. Gabriel, how do you know Lester was pleased? Don't tell me you both went."

"Yes."

"Where was Lester staying then?"

Gabriel began to describe the almost invisible hotel but Mum wasn't listening; she was looking closely at him.

"I know you've seen Lester," she said. "You've still got some of my eye shadow on. Isn't that right?"

"Green's our color, I think."

"Not that vulgar green." She said, "Nothing will come of any of it."

"Maybe. But he said I'm talented."

"Show business people always talk such shit. They said it about your father once. Funky fingers. Butter fingers more like."

"I didn't get the impression," said Gabriel with the pomposity of a headmaster, "that he was only trying to be kind."

"Oh, didn't you. What picture are you talking about? Show it to me. It doesn't exist."

"Christine!" A voice called from downstairs. "We want some more!"

Gabriel said, "Who's that?"

"A friend. I should go."

Gabriel got out of bed and unrolled the picture. He held it out for her and she looked at it for a long time.

"It *is* by him. Where are you going to keep it?"

"Dad really likes it. It'll cheer up his room."

"Does it need cheering up?"

"He hasn't even got a picture of Archie."

"Hasn't he? I'm not sure he even thinks about Archie now."

Gabriel said, "The walls are so greasy at Dad's place I doubt whether anything will stick to them."

"You can't put it there, then. Oh no, no, no."

"But I'll frame it first."

"You said it's bleak over there, didn't you?"

"Christine!" called a different voice.

"Who's that?"

"Another friend."

"Mum, couldn't you go round to Dad's and do some dusting?"

"Oh yes," she said sarcastically. "First thing in the morning. He's got plenty of time on his hands, hasn't he?"

"Don't you want to see him?"

"Why should I?"

"He's in bad shape." She said nothing. "I think he wants to see you."

She said, "He's not working, is he?"

"Not at the moment. He's busy . . . thinking."

She pretended to choke. "He's what?"

Gabriel repeated, "Thinking things over."

"Thinking! Ha, ha, ha!" She was laughing hard. She repeated the word several times. "Thinking!" Each time she said it she howled unnaturally.

At last she picked up the picture. "I'm going to borrow this."

"Mum—"

"I want to show it to my friends, d'you have any objection?"

"Dad's helping me think what to do with it."

"I bet he is," she said. "What suggestions does he have?"

"I don't know yet."

"He won't be doing anything with it tonight, surely. Nor ever, if I have my way."

"What?"

She said, "Please let them look."

"As long as they don't breathe on it."

"Don't worry, these characters are hardly alive at all."

She took the picture and swept from the room.

Gabriel put on his slippers and hurried out behind her.

It was almost dark in the living room but Gabriel could see that his mother's two friends were emptying bottles down their throats and the front of their shirts as rapidly as they could.

The door to the little kitchen was open; Hannah's flickering black and white television illuminated the outline of her solid peasant frame wrapped in a blanket.

The two men were arguing.

"The thing is—" one of them was saying.

"That's not the case at all," the other was saying. "In fact you are talking complete crap—"

"I'm going to convince you, George," said the other, offering his fist. "Sit still and hear me out now."

Like a teacher addressing a group of school kids, Mum held the picture out.

"Look—you bums. Look at this. This is by Lester Jones, the pop star. I used to know him. I designed him a pair of flocked trousers. We called it his 'Indian Restaurant' period."

"But listen—" said the man called George.

"I know exactly what you're going to say," said the other. "And if you say it, I'll fight to the death not to have to hear it—"

Mum snapped the music off, cleared the ashtrays and glasses off the table, and laid the picture out.

She pointed at Gabriel.

"This is him, my son."

One of the men said, "I'd forgotten you'd said you had one of those."

The other said, "What the hell is he wearing?"

Mum said, "A kimono. Never mind that. Now, Gabriel, Lester Jones drew this for you, isn't that right?"

"Not entirely, Mum. Dad's an old friend of Lester's. Lester told me that Dad was one of the best musicians he played with. Dad created his sound, really. Lester had started the picture already and when Dad and I turned up—"

"All right, all right. You're not giving a lecture at the Tate Gallery. Did you know, Lester Jones had me once," she said. "Years ago. I think he wanted to go out with me."

"You should have married him," one of the men said.

"At least I wouldn't have to buy my own drinks!"

"And you wouldn't be hanging around with us," said the other man.

"Now," she said, "look at it, you two."

Trying to be obedient, the two men attempted to focus on the picture, one of them busily rubbing his eyes for a clearer view.

After a time one of them said, "What is it?"

The other replied, "Never mind that—"

"He should stick to singing."

"Look at it, for Christ's sake," said Mum. "That's all I'm asking you to do."

One man elbowed the other, to shut him up. They gazed at the picture mournfully, saying nothing until the glowing ash from one man's cigarette dropped, like a desiccated leaf, onto the paper. Gabriel, who had been watching, leapt forward, flicking it away before it could mark the picture. The ash flew into the other man's lap.

He regretted it; the picture would have made a pretty conflagration. The fire might have caught him too. Mum would have had to put him out, wrapping him in sheets like a mummy. He would have had many restful weeks in bed. Why was it so pleasurable to think of destroying the most valuable things?

"OK," said his mother. "That's enough! Another time!" She turned to the men. "He's talented, you know."

"Lester can sing, no doubt about that. 'Ha, ha said the clown!'"

"That's not him," said the other man. Gabriel could smell the ash smoldering in the front of the man's trousers. "That's—"

Mum said, "No, I mean Gabriel!"

"Who?" said the man with the burning trousers. By now his eyes were wide and he was holding his crotch with one hand and flapping in it with the other.

"This boy—this boy right in front of you!"

The men looked at Gabriel the apparition. Usually, when his mother became angry, Gabriel and his father grew afraid. But these men were unmoved and looked at her vacantly. They seemed to have taken something, not only alcohol, that made them not understand what was going on. This mystified Gabriel; he knew something about drugs—every kid did these days—but he still didn't know why anyone would want to do this to themselves.

She turned to Gabriel: "Hey, I've got an idea. Show them how talented you are! Will you draw us? Yes, all of us—here, now! Go and get your crayons and stuff. What a good idea!"

"I don't feel like it, Mum. I'm tired and I've got school tomorrow! I should be in bed!"

"That's the first time you've ever said that! Don't be sulky."

"Couldn't I just sing 'Consider Yourself'?"

"What for? We've got music here. Too good for us, are you, now that Lester has praised you?"

"Go on," said one of the men.

The other man laughed. "Get a job, lad!"

Gabriel went upstairs and fetched his things.

When he came back he settled down in a corner of the room, and soon his mother and her fuzzy-eyed friends, drinking, yelling and retiring to the bathroom to do something secret, seemed to forget him.

He drew quickly, as he liked to now, in crayon, rubbing the colors together with his finger, to give the impression of the smoke-smudged room. For some reason the scene reminded him of an artist he liked, Toulouse-Lautrec, who had, by the age of sixteen, completed fifty paintings and three hundred drawings. Once Gabriel had recalled this, Lautrec's was the style he worked in.

After a time his mother remembered him. "Let's have a look! Is it good?"

She carried the sketchbook across the room and turned on a reading light.

For some time she studied the picture of the tired, middle-aged, black-stockinged woman pulling her skirts up, while corpulent, self-important men in tight waistcoats looked on condescendingly.

Standing next to her, Gabriel noticed she wasn't wearing the Indian ring Dad had given her. It wasn't a wedding ring—as bourgeois as tradesmen in every other way, they weren't of a generation that got married. Dad had bought it the day he took Mum to the Taj Mahal: "Not the restaurant, the building in India," it gave him pleasure to explain. Gabriel had never seen her without it before.

He was about to mention this when one of the men said, "The tension is killing us—let's have a look!"

He went to Gabriel's mother, put his arm around her and lifted her arse. Gabriel didn't like the way he touched her, but couldn't wait to see what the man made of the picture.

The man laughed and turned back to Gabriel. "Couldn't you have made me more handsome, you little devil? I look like a wild boar!"

"I wonder why!" said the other man.

"Look at what he's done with you!" said the first. "Microwaved pizza comes to mind!"

His mother took the picture, folded it up, and put it on the table.

"Aren't you going to bed, Mum?" Gabriel said.

"Yes, yes, soon."

She accompanied Gabriel upstairs to bed, forgetting to kiss him because she was thinking hard about something else.

"Dad wouldn't like these people," Gabriel said.

"It's none of his business. Nothing is, now."

Much later the front door slammed. A man's voice echoed up the street; then a bottle smashed. She went into her room and everything was quiet again.

Hearing a whimpering noise, Gabriel went out onto the landing. Her door was open.

She was sitting up on the high bed wearing nothing but her knickers and one shoe. Mum must have been weary; she could hardly sit up. One of her arms, pressing against the bed, kept giving way. Her other hand was between her thighs.

Gabriel heard a voice but couldn't tell, at first, where it was coming from. At last he realized that one of the men was sitting on the floor with his head on his chest, singing to himself and trying to take his shirt off.

Gabriel encouraged him to stand up.

"That's George's," slurred the man, pointing at the bed. "I will climb up there in a bit and conquer. First I want the toilet."

"This way," said Gabriel. "Give me your shirt."

"Thank you, sir. You aren't, by any chance, a shirt-lifter?"

"No."

Before the man knew where he was, Gabriel had led him downstairs, opened the front door and pushed him out onto the freezing street. He quickly locked the door behind him and turned the lights off.

Watching the man unbutton his fly in the middle of the road, Gabriel shouted through the letter box. "It's an outside toilet! There, on the left! Don't forget to flush it! Mind that car behind you!"

He had never seen Mum this drunk. As she subsided Gabriel saw she was about to drop down onto the floor. He climbed the ladder, put his arms around her and dragged her heavy body further onto the bed. She didn't seem to notice him pulling her into her pajama jacket but as he did up the buttons she started to kiss him and call him "darling."

"But it's Gabriel," he said.

Her mouth was open; she was already breathing heavily.

He could have drawn her. Not that he needed to fetch his sketchbook; it was a scene he would remember.

Gabriel covered her up and kissed her goodnight.

Six

Next morning Gabriel was up before his mother, preparing for school while Hannah soldered the scrambled eggs to the side of the frying pan and torched the toast.

"How's the picture?"

Dad was already on the phone. From where he stood, Gabriel could see a man's shirt hanging over the back of a chair.

"Fine."

"Finished with it?"

"Not yet."

"Mum see it?"

"Yes."

"How come?"

Gabriel said, "She's nosy. She finds things."

"Yes," said Dad. "Did she like it?"

"Quite."

"What did you tell her?" Dad asked. "Did you mention Lester?"

"Yes. Is that OK? She was impressed by that, Dad."

"I'm sure. You didn't tell her anything bad about me?"

"Like what? No."

Dad sighed. "You're keeping the picture safe? Is it right there beside you?"

"Oh yes. It's right here. In fact . . . I'm looking at it!"

"Call me when you're ready. Maybe I'll pick it up later today, after school." Dad added politely, "Is that fine by you?"

Gabriel said, "What else are you doing today, Dad?"

"I don't know yet. We'll have to see what develops."

"Where's Lester's picture?" Gabriel asked Hannah, biting into a charcoal and peanut butter mixture. "Have you seen it?"

She looked at him in bewilderment. She didn't know what he was talking about.

The last time Gabriel had seen the picture, it was on the living room table. But it wasn't there anymore. His mother had probably taken it into her own room for safekeeping. She wouldn't thank him for going in there and waking her up.

He went to school but didn't pay attention to his lessons. He was beginning to think he was too old for school, or the school itself was somehow backward, or too old-fashioned for him. It didn't give him enough to think about. As soon as he began to concentrate on a piece of schoolwork, he became aware that more exciting things were going on somewhere else.

That morning, catching him jotting film ideas in his notebook before he forgot them, Gabriel's teacher snatched away the notebook, saying, "Why aren't you concentrating, Gabriel Bunch?"

"It's not interesting enough to keep my attention, sir," he replied, without thinking.

"Not interesting enough! What do you think this is—an entertainment?"

"If only, sir. If only."

The other kids were laughing.

The teacher said, "I'll come down on you like a pile of bricks."

One of the other kids yelled, "The customer is always right, sir!"

Someone else chipped in, "One size fits all! One fit sizes all!"

"Always follow the instructions!"

"Don't try this at home!"

"Look away now!"

"We're on our way to Wembley!"

It was a madhouse.

Gabriel looked at the teacher and replied, "That's all you are, sir. A big pile of bricks."

"Repeat that, Bunch."

It was the only instruction Gabriel felt happy to follow.

The teacher refrained from striking him, but Gabriel was supposed to be in detention for a week. Not that he would turn up. Zak, who read a lot and used difficult words (he could even spell "precocious"), had said not to worry, the system lacked imagination and was so coercive that failure was the only distinction; conformity was a kind of death. And as Dad pointed out, it was supposed to be a school, not a lunatic asylum, and certainly not a prison.

Gabriel had been sent out of the schoolroom, and stood alone in the corridor, like a dog forced to wait outside a shop for its owner.

"Fascism," Zak had mouthed, passing by. "Ring me."

"I will," Gabriel replied.

At school, he and Zak were now in different classes and barely met. To keep out of trouble for being middle-class, Zak had had to become a librarian. Books, he had discovered, were good for hiding behind. Adults respected books, though no one had explained why.

Zak was bright; he took things in. He could work things out for himself, too. "Parents are funny," he said once. "What do they want from us? Our respect and for us to listen. But do they bother to respect us? How often do they listen to us and think about what we want?"

School didn't interest Zak either. He put up with it because he knew he was just passing through. He could see how much there was ahead of him.

Gabriel had hardly seen Zak out of school since his father had left. Zak knew what had taken place—the same thing had happened to him, as it had to several others in the class. To be part of a "complete" family was, these days, to be in a minority. But Gabriel hadn't wanted to talk about the breakup. Words were as dangerous as bombs, as Gabriel discovered when he swore in front of his mother. They didn't only describe; they did things to other people, or made things happen, and more than enough was happening at the moment.

Anyway, children understood tyrannies, he thought, living with those vicious moody bosses called parents, under a regime in which their thoughts and activities were severely constrained. The kids were anarchists and dissidents, operating underground, in secret cells, trying to find an inviolable privacy.

At that moment he didn't feel like a glorious anarchist.

A passing teacher who had hardly addressed more than a handful of phrases to him, stopped for a moment and said, "I remember you, Bunch. That is your name, isn't it?"

"Yes, sir."

"When you arrived here you were full of confidence. Now you look scared all the time." The teacher touched his face. "That twitch of yours has come back."

"Has it, sir?"

Gabriel had had a twitch in one eye, which flickered like a faulty camera shutter. When he was made conscious of it, it felt as if his face was inhabited by spiders; insects were rushing beneath his skin.

"Look after yourself," the teacher said.

"Thank you, sir."

He would look after himself. The experience with Lester had taken him into another world, where he seemed to belong. He couldn't wait to remind himself of it by examining the picture again.

That afternoon, when he got home, he couldn't find it anywhere, not in his mother's room, and not in his own.

He turned out cupboards and looked in the same place again and again, before going to Hannah, who was standing outside the bathroom.

"Sorry, Hannah," he said in a businesslike voice. "I've got to go out to a meeting. I'd be grateful if you'd keep my supper warm."

"I'll warm your arse in a minute!" When necessary Hannah could find the appropriate phrase. She had made friends with other au pairs; in some ways, as London became richer, it was becoming more Victorian. Her friends must have been coaching her. "It's bath time! Water all over!"

She pointed at the full bath.

"*You* get in," he said. "You could do with a wash!"

She was even more shocked when he put his coat on, took the man's shirt from the back of a chair, and went out of the house, announcing, "What a lovely evening for a stroll!"

She stood on the doorstep and cried in reasonable English, "Wait, wait! I am in charge!"

"I'm going to see Mum," he said. "I'm not a child."

When he looked back he saw that she was intending to start off behind him, but it didn't take him long to lose her.

His mother worked several streets away, and he was soon there.

The bar became raucous after work, filling up with office workers in black clothes. At the door a waitress tried to stop him. "You're too young!"

"Put me in jail."

He saw his mother across the room, standing at a table beside a man he recognized without knowing where from. It was strange: she was the most important woman in his life, and unimportant here, just another waitress. Worse, at that moment she probably wasn't thinking of him.

"Mum!" He was standing on tiptoe.

At his voice she looked up. He could, suddenly, command her attention and make her his again. It was a wonderful power.

She hurried over. "Is something wrong?"

"Yes."

"What is it? Tell me! Are you not well?" She pressed her hand to his forehead. "You are hot!"

"Course I'm hot! Where's my picture? The one Lester gave me."

"Oh, that. Is that why you've come? What's that in your hand?"

"The shirt one of those sweaty men left last night."

She took it and folded it up a little too neatly for his liking. She said, "I've put the picture away for safekeeping."

"Thanks. But I want it now."

"What for?"

"That's up to me."

"Don't shout at me. I'm a single mother and I've got a headache!"

"I'm surprised you can stand up at all."

She had her hurt face on, making him feel that it was his fault, that his demands were unreasonable.

The waitress who had tried to stop him coming in went up to his mother. "Christine, there's a customer waiting."

"Coming." To Gabriel, Mum said, "Go home."

He said, "I want to look at it."

"Don't mess it up. It'll get damaged with everyone pulling at it."

"You mean Dad?"

"That man's an old hippie. They were a generation that didn't want to understand the value of things. Why d'you think we've been poor all these years? Dad didn't want to be 'materialistic.' Where I've put the picture . . . it'll be safe. You can have it—of course you can have it—when you're older."

"Older! Will I never be the right age? I was old enough when he gave it to me. It's mine and that's a fact."

"A fact? A fact!" she laughed. "But we're family."

"A family!"

"We can look at it as a family, when I say."

Gabriel said, "I want Dad to look at it sometimes, too."

"I'll think about that. He's gone. He doesn't want us. Why d'you think he walked out?"

Gabriel was shaking; he hated her and was afraid of his own fury. She refused to understand him, or take him seriously. She was even angry with his anger.

"What I notice," she said as they walked to the door, "is how you come here only when you want something for yourself. Why, when I saw you, I almost thought you had come in to see how I'm getting on!"

"How are you getting on?"

"What? Fine," she said. "I like it here. Your father once told me that I have the mind of a waitress. Maybe he was right, eh?"

He looked up to see the black post-box of Hannah heaving through the door.

"Bad, bad boy."

She almost collapsed and had to lean against a table.

"Thank you, Hannah," said his mother, returning to her work.

"Boy," said Hannah. "Boy—come here."

Outside, Hannah took his hand and tried to pull him across the road as though he were a short-legged child. He stumbled along behind her, reminded of being dragged by his mother and slapped on the legs by her as an infant.

At the edge of the pavement he stopped and wrenched his hand away from her; if she touched him, he would flatten her and take the consequences.

Hannah was looking at him: his eyes must have blazed; there was fear in hers.

"OK, OK," she said. "Follow up." She started off in one direction, and then in another.

"Which way?" he asked.

"Oh, I don't know," she said. "Where are we?"

"London." He added, "You'd better follow me."

Turning the corner at the end of their street, Gabriel saw that Dad was standing outside the house. Gabriel took Hannah's hand and pulled her behind a van.

"I'm staying here," he whispered. "You go to the house. Let him see you."

Hannah was perplexed but did what he said. When Dad saw her approaching, he walked away quickly and turned the corner without looking back.

Later, Gabriel searched for the picture again but couldn't find it. He became increasingly annoyed with his mother and decided to wait until she returned, and interrogate her later. But when she came in he heard a man's voice and decided to wait until the front door slammed. By that time, however, he was exhausted and had fallen asleep.

Seven

He awoke as suddenly as if he had been shaken. He switched the light on and looked about. There was no other hand in the room. He wondered whether he had been dreaming about death, as he used to. But it wasn't that: he wasn't sweating and frightened.

He seemed to hear a voice in the distance. At first, he thought it was his father outside the house, wanting to be let in. However, when he listened he knew it was Archie, calling to him. Archie had an announcement.

"What is it, Archie?" said Gabriel in a low voice. "I'm here if you've got something to say. You better spit it out, little brother—I'm not hanging around."

Archie began to speak.

He told Gabriel where the picture was and that he should fetch it. Had there been two of them, he said, that was what they'd do, have an adventure, like the twins in Enid Blyton's stories. Except that there was a little problem. Archie informed Gabriel that Lester's picture was hidden in their mother's bedroom, and of course Mum was asleep.

Archie didn't seem bothered by this. Ordinary obstacles didn't burden wraiths.

Once Archie had said where the picture was, Gabriel knew his brother was right; that was where it would be. He should have thought of it himself. Mum had no imagination when it came to hiding things. Or perhaps she underestimated his determination.

What determination?

He was sitting there in the cold and dark. The only sound was of Hannah snoring: the wind of her restless breath whipped under the door and froze his ankles. He wanted to slip under his duvet and go to sleep. But although he cursed Archie's sense of humor, he couldn't deny the dead boy's percipience.

Gabriel had to follow the angel voice where it led.

He smoked half a joint, opened his door, went out of his room and stood on the landing. His mother's door was always ajar: since he and Archie had been babies, she had left the door open to hear them if they cried.

He pushed her door and stepped into the darkness. He was in her room; he could hear her breathing. He took one more step before hitting an invisible wall and finding himself suspended in space. He landed on the floor.

Reaching out, he realized he had tripped over some shoes, big shoes like blocks of wood. These were not his mother's. Her shoes, as well he knew, were always in a row under the window.

He was lying on the floor of her bedroom, still as a corpse and about as merry, holding his breath. At least he was facedown on the floor where he wanted to be. If she opened her eyes, she wouldn't see him, though she might, of course, smell him.

As he listened he realized someone was in bed with her. Not

only might she wake up, but the other person—whoever it was—might too, and there'd be four angry eyes condemning him.

There was enough light for Gabriel to drag himself across the floor until he reached the stanchions that supported the bed. He knew his way around under there. Children always noticed the underneath of things; for a long time, like foot soldiers and servants, they only saw the world from below, a good position for noticing how things worked.

The metal drawer was padlocked but the combination lock had given before, when he'd pulled and twisted it. Except he had to do it silently now. He worked as slowly and carefully as he could, but it refused to give way. He felt like crying. How could he ever guess the combination? He remained still and thought hard, before trying—as Archie seemed to be advising—the last four digits of their phone number. It didn't work. Then he tried the year of his and Archie's birth. Weren't most mothers sentimental? The lock opened. He was in. He pulled the drawer.

The rolled-up picture was there, as Archie had said it would be. Gabriel had it in his hand. All he had to do now was get out without being noticed. That shouldn't be too difficult.

As he went to move there were hushed voices and even giggles; then the springs started a vigorous vibration. He didn't think he'd make it across the room and out of the door without being spotted. He'd have to wait. The wooden bed legs were aching by now; in fact they seemed to be groaning, cracking and preparing to give way. Everything could come down with him underneath! He put his hands over his ears. It was terrifying but Archie was holding onto him.

Two in the bed, two under it, their lives living out, this night; and Dad in his room, not far away. Was he awake too?

When it was silent again, and the couple's normal breathing had resumed, Gabriel crawled out and carried the picture into his room, where he laid it out on his table.

What did he see in it? One big face and other, little faces; animals, lines, colors, movement. Obscure things trying to become clear. It was busy; there was a lot in it, as there was in Lester's music, with a memorable melody at the front that everyone could enjoy.

This was a good way to look at a picture, or at anything, as if you were about to draw it yourself.

He went to his art cupboard.

Night passed. He stayed up until the morning, working. He had to cover the mirror again because when he looked into it he didn't see his own reflection but that of Archie, a face the same as Gabriel's but detectably different in ways he couldn't have described, though perhaps Archie's eyes were slightly further apart than Gabriel's. Gabriel thought of a Plath poem he'd read at school, called "Mirror." "I am not cruel," it went, "only truthful—/ The eye of a little god, four-cornered."

To keep him awake, Archie sang to him, Mozart, Sinatra, Ella and Joe Cocker. With Archie's hand on his, he copied the picture—twice. Gabriel was used to copying; he knew how to do it, and he enjoyed it. Now there'd be enough art to go round; no one would be left out!

In the morning, Mum called him downstairs. "Gabriel, breakfast!"

A man was sitting at the table in the living room, dropping his ash into a saucer. Gabriel had to sit down.

"This is George," said Mum. "George, Gabriel. Don't you remember?"

They shook hands.

Mum was whispering at George about the bar and some dispute she was having with the people there. Then she sent Hannah to the market and went to get ready.

"Is there any more tea?" George asked.

In this light George looked younger than Gabriel remembered, in his early thirties, with long dark hair and haughty upper-class features.

Gabriel sniffed. "I think so."

"Would you fetch me some? I don't feel too well. I almost caught pneumonia the other night."

"How come?"

"I don't remember."

Gabriel went into the kitchen and made some tea. He was tired; it had been a long night and he had to go to school.

Turning up the radio, he cleared his throat, put his head back and spat in George's tea. Though he added milk and sugar, and stirred it, the snot-green tea still looked noxious.

George was so exhausted his head was almost on the table.

Gabriel gave him the drink and sat opposite him.

"What are you doing today, George?"

"Oh, I don't know. I'm a painter, so I don't have to do anything except sit on my arse. Don't you like artists?"

"Mum always says they're no-good people."

"She's never said that to me."

"Not yet," said Gabriel. "There's a lot of things people don't say at first. She doesn't like to be tied down, for instance. More than anything she likes her freedom. And I'm her favorite boy."

George said, "The poor woman's tired. She's been run off her feet lately."

"Really. Enjoying your tea?"

"Thanks, yes."

"More sugar?"

"No."

"Milk?"

The phone rang.

"How are you, Dad?" said Gabriel.

"Is your mother there?"

"Do you want to talk to her?"

Dad hesitated. "I don't mind."

"She's in the shower."

Dad seemed relieved. "You and I can talk then. Can I have the picture?"

"I'm nearly finished with it."

"Good. I'll come and pick it up."

How keen people became when they wanted something!

"Yes," said Gabriel. "Whenever you like but definitely not now. Not until I tell you when."

George sipped his tea and started to cough and choke. "Christ Almighty!" he said. "Can't breathe!"

"Who's that?" said Dad.

"Hannah."

"What is she, a baritone?"

"Yes."

"I bet. Let me talk to that guy."

"Don't be stupid, Dad."

"Listen, you've got to help me out. Don't be too long with the picture," said Dad.

"What's the problem?"

"As well as being a bit short of cash, I haven't got long to live!"

"Are you not well?"

"Going down. On the way to zero."

His father replaced the receiver.

Gabriel said to George, "That was my dad. He's coming round."

"Now?"

"He could be. He's a musician."

George snorted. "He used to be."

"You never lose a talent—if you're fortunate enough to have one in the first place."

When Mum came in, George said, "Gabriel's explaining to me about talent."

"Oh yes. He would know."

Gabriel said, "Dad had an incredible talent, but something terrible happened to him."

"Yes, I heard he fell flat on his face," said George. "Everyone knows."

Gabriel said, "Shall I tell him about Dad's dream about being asked to join the Rolling Stones, but as a cleaner? He had to sweep peanuts from the stage as they played. Then, back-stage—"

"Let's leave that," said his mother. "George is a painter."

George was smiling at her. "I'm going to paint you, my dear."

"I don't know."

"You agreed."

"I'm not confident enough," she said.

"You're a coy little thing, aren't you?"

"But I am shy. You know I am, George."

"I do. But you're not always shy, my darling. I'm thinking of the other night when you—"

"Stop it now, please."

George said, "Look at these, Gabriel."

"He's too young, George."

"Rubbish. Boys of his age are more experienced than we are. I'm not too old to remember!"

George produced a bag and some slides. Gabriel went to the window and held them up to the light. There were paintings of near-naked, completely naked and obscenely naked women with Pre-Raphaelite hair made of swirls and flurries of irrele-vant paint.

"You're in PR then," said Gabriel.

"What are you saying now, Gabriel?" asked his mother. She said to George, "He's always bloody well saying something funny."

"Pre-Raphaelites." Gabriel cleared his throat. "Lots of color."

"You like them?" asked George.

"I like looking at things," said Gabriel.

"You like girls?"

"Sometimes."

"Got a girlfriend?"

"I had five. No one at the moment."

"Why's that?"

"I haven't had time to develop a meaningful relationship."

"George, don't tease him," said Mum. "George works in Italy. In a castle on a hill. He's invited us to go and see him there. We can stay as long as we like."

George said, "The Tiber valley. It's not far from where the Giottos fell on the monks' heads. God's joke, I think. My district is full of artists and writers. In the evening, when the day has cooled down, we sit in the little square. The local carpenter puts up a screen, and we watch films outdoors, smoking, drinking and arguing until late."

Gabriel nodded.

George pointed at the wall. "Looks as though some of these old photographs have been up too long. Who's that other boy?"

"He died a long time ago," said Mum. "He was Gabriel's twin."

"God Almighty, so there were two of them?" said George.

"Yes," said Mum. "There were. Now there aren't."

She was biting her lip.

Gabriel said, "Elvis was a twin. Then he blew up to twice his own size."

"Really?" said George. To Christine he said, "Would you like a picture?"

"Oh yes," said Mum.

"Gabriel?"

"As long as it matches the wallpaper."

George was laughing.

Gabriel said, "Do you just paint or do you decorate as well?"

George's color changed. Mum looked at Gabriel. "I think we should have a talk," she said.

"I'm ready," he said.

"Christine—" said George. "I thought we were going out to breakfast."

"All right." She said to Gabriel, "I didn't mean now. You've got to go to school. We will talk, another time."

"I'll put it in my diary," said Gabriel.

"He's got a lot of lip," said George. "If I had a stapler, I'd pin his lips together."

"Yes. Stop it, Gabriel."

"Stop what?"

"Whatever you're doing."

When George and Mum had left the house—and Gabriel watched them going down the road, talking and laughing together—Gabriel returned to his two copies. He was pleased with them; he had done what he had set out to do.

To celebrate, he took his big music box into the "garden"— a concrete patio enclosed by a fence topped with barbed wire— and danced and sang until he fell over.

Afterwards, he rolled up one copy of the picture and placed it under his mother's bed, clicking home the padlock and rolling the wheels of the combination. He put the original and one copy in a cupboard no one ever looked in, that was full of old toys and books.

He didn't think his mother would bother to look at the picture under the bed, as she was so preoccupied with her job and George and her friends.

However, that evening she came into his room.

"I know you're concerned about your precious picture, Angel," she said. "But I came home when you were at school, picked it up from where I'd put it away for safekeeping, and took it to work."

"To the bar?"

"To show people."

"To show off," he muttered.

"Sorry?"

He said, "Mum . . . did they like it?"

"They thought it excellent."

"The colors . . . they approved of?"

"I told them all about how I designed Lester's trousers, and who I would hang out with in those cafés and restaurants in Chelsea. Most of the kitchen kids are too young to recognize the names of the people I knew, of course. I was unappreciated, as usual. Some of them, though, had some good suggestions about what to do with the picture."

"What d'you mean?"

"How to show it off to its full advantage. Meanwhile, I'm going to put it away again," she said. She was puzzled when she looked at him. "You're not going to make one of your fusses, are you?"

"No, Mum. As long as it's safe. That's all that matters. I know you know how to look after things."

"Yes," she said, a little skeptically. "Good boy."

His mind palpitated with pride. He thought of everyone looking at the picture. It had been his copy of Lester's picture that they had praised in the bar. His scheme had worked; no one had suspected a thing. His mother was happy and so was he.

He had become, in a way, an appreciated artist, though as anonymous, for the time being, as one of Rubens's assistants.

Eight

The next time his father rang, Gabriel said he had sufficiently studied and thought about the picture. Now he was ready to lend it out. He said, "I'll bring it to you after school, Dad. I can remember where you live."

"Whatever you do, don't go walking about with that work of art. You might drop it! Take it easy right where you are. I'm coming to get it—now. Are you sure you've 'studied' it enough?"

"Well, I think I—"

Before Gabriel could reply, Dad replaced the receiver. Later that morning he was smiling on the doorstep.

"What are you going to do with it?" said Gabriel, bringing out the picture and handing it to him. Gabriel felt both proud of and guilty about the copy.

"It's going on the wall! Gabriel, you're an angel!" Dad opened it out and was looking at it. "It's even better than I remember."

Dad kissed the picture.

Gabriel said, "Don't you want me to help you get it framed and put up?"

"No thanks!"

"But you haven't even got a hammer!"

"Don't worry about that—I'll use my dick!"

Gabriel said, "Why are you in such a hurry? Don't you want to have a chat?"

"Later. Things are starting to look up. Cheerio."

Gabriel watched his father cycling up the road with the picture inside his jacket.

Gabriel didn't hear from him again; he guessed his father was busy starting a new life. However, a few days later Hannah, on his mother's instructions, was deputed to accompany Gabriel to his father's house, where he was to spend the afternoon.

Hannah, who stood on the doorstep in her vast black overcoat, heavy shoes and hat, looked like someone from another age. But at least she had sartorial self-respect, thought Gabriel. The rest of the older population now resembled a legion of disoriented mountaineers, in lightweight, all-weather clothes covered in pockets, with labels like Eiger and South Face.

"Come on, then," he said, helping her down the steps. "And make sure I don't fall into the clutches of any drug dealers on the way."

Hannah rarely went further than the local shops and market. As Gabriel led her to the bus stop and saw how alarmed she was by the swirling indifferent crowd and its numerous languages, he talked to her continuously. Still she insisted on taking his hand; not, he realized, to lead him, but for fear of getting lost herself.

Seeing the various neighborhoods from her point of view—for a while it seemed advantageous to pretend to himself that he was in Calcutta—he noticed that the bus, onto which they had had to clamber at the traffic lights as the driver appeared to see no other reason for slowing down, was driven by a monosyllabic lunatic who only stopped when shouted at by the passengers, most of whom were listening to music on headphones. Other "customers" chatted loudly on their mobiles and almost everyone else gibbered and swore to themselves. Then the bus—because of road works, he was told—didn't take its usual route but seemed to veer around West London almost at random, with the frantic passengers shouting instructions each time they saw a sign saying DIVERSION.

She was solid, Hannah, and, back on the street, moved only slowly, with a kind of shuffle, whereas everyone else was engulfed by the stream; a moment's hesitation could engender a homicide. Gabriel tried to stand between her and this eventuality.

By the time they reached Dad's house she seemed exhausted. But when, on the pavement outside, she heard people speaking in her language, Hannah's face brightened and she started to follow them into the building. Gabriel had to tell her to stay where she was.

"Why—?" she began.

"Dad might be in a bad mood," he explained.

She stepped back sadly. Gabriel couldn't let her see Dad's place for fear she wouldn't be able to resist telling his mother that he was drinking beer, surrounded by ashtrays, dirty plates, and his only asset, a picture by an old rock star.

Gabriel then took her to the bus stop, accompanied her onto the ship of fools and instructed someone to tell her when to get off. Then, as she looked so bewildered, and he was grateful not to be her, he bent down to her face and kissed her. Her hands went to his and she kissed him back, in gratitude. He waved from the street as her terrified face flew into the traffic.

At last he was pushing on his father's door.

"Here comes the son!" called Dad gaily. He was in bed in all his clothes, apart from his trousers, reading the paper. "Little darlin'!"

"You're cheerful today," said Gabriel. "What are we going

to do? Is it a museum or the cinema? There's a film I want to see." He patted his pocket. "Don't worry, Mum's given me the money."

"Why—does she think I haven't got any?"

"She knows you, Dad."

"And she thinks I'm useless. If we want to see a film we can do it. We can go anywhere we like—almost."

"How come?"

"You'll see. Pass me my trousers. Have you noticed that they're new combats?"

Gabriel was looking around. "Where's Lester's picture?"

His father got up energetically but slipped on several discarded beer cans and landed back on the bed.

Gabriel helped him up and said, "Take it easy, Dad. Save the falls for a stadium."

"When I find the motherfucking floor and my shoes I'm going to show you where your picture is."

"We have to go somewhere? You said it was on the wall."

"It is on the wall. Not on this wall, necessarily. But it is definitely on a wall. A wall is a wall, isn't it? Or are you picky about your walls?"

"I am picky about them, as it happens. I like my possessions to be on walls I know."

"Do you want to see it or not?"

"I'm less keen now."

Dad was putting his trousers on. "Christ, you're in a dismal mood."

"You've put me in one, funky fingers," said Gabriel.

"You'll be OK in a minute. Got any grass?"

"I've given up, Dad."

"Mum tell you off?"

"It was making me paranoid . . . and I kept seeing strange things. Chairs and stuff."

"Yeah, I've had paranoia in my time. No chairs, though. I

wouldn't want that. Chairs? Was it the stuff you got at school or the stuff I grew at home?"

"All of it. I've been getting very lost in my own head and sometimes I feel I'll never get out, as if I'm—"

"Come on now, we've got things to do."

As they went out, Gabriel noticed, leaning against the entrance, the man with the curly slippers who'd threatened Dad. He nodded as they went past, as if he knew everything about them.

After traveling a short distance, Dad locked up the bicycle and they walked to a hamburger restaurant with a flashing neon sign announcing the name, Splitz.

The girl on the door greeted Dad like a friend, kissing him on both cheeks.

"What sort of place is this?" Gabriel said. "What are we doing here?"

"Speedy—the boss and owner—is an old pal. He used to hang around the bands. When we were on tour, he started to cook for us. He was so slow because he couldn't stop wittering on that he was called Speedy. Look at him now, shaking his withered old pussy in cream while we're just—just creamed!"

Gabriel looked at tourists and adolescents in London for the day, eating hamburgers as big as rugby balls, knickerbocker glories and sundaes like icebergs.

"But Dad—"

Dad said, "Yo! Speedy!"

Hurtling towards them, Speedy was middle-aged with a young man's face, tinted yellow. He had good teeth and teenage American clothes.

"This is him, my boy," said Dad.

"At last," said Speedy. He took Gabriel's hand and caressed it with long, manicured fingers. "He is blond, and not the wrong blond either! Those cheekbones could cut you open! Where did he get them?"

"Not from me, obviously," said Dad.

"And Lester's friend, too! I can see why."

Speedy laughed soundlessly by opening his mouth and pushing his head forward on its long wrinkled neck. Gabriel guessed that professionally he had to laugh a lot and this was the most economical way to do it.

"How is dear Lester?" Speedy asked.

On closer examination, Gabriel saw that Speedy's head seemed to have been shrunken from a larger model, as if his features had shriveled over the years.

"The very same cool dude," said Dad. "I told you, I was hanging out with him just the other day. You know, when he gave me the . . . thing."

"Thing?"

"The thing . . . on the wall."

"Yes, yes. That reminds me, there's something I need to tell you. Hold on a minute."

"Bacchus with a face-lift," whispered Dad, as Speedy suddenly disappeared to have his lips nibble at another face.

On his return, Speedy said, "Come up to my operating table."

They climbed the underlit stairs to a table set on a dais overlooking the restaurant, covered in papers, magazines, invitations and CDs. A waitress brought them milkshakes and beer.

"Now," said Speedy, rubbing his hands together. "I'll show you."

"I can't wait," said Dad. To Gabriel he said, "I haven't seen it yet! I didn't want to look without you."

"You'll be ecstatic," said Speedy. "This picture looks good!"

"Sorry?" said Gabriel.

"Quiet," said Dad, picking up his beer glass. "Just wait and see, will you, Gabriel!" He said to Speedy, "He's very impatient."

"Good for him," said Speedy. "If you ask me, nothing you have to wait for is worth having."

Gabriel was led past a wall on which hung gold discs and tour jackets; some of the jackets might have been made by his mother. There were photographs of menacing young men in ostentatious "Saturday" clothes, boys who were once heroes to other boys. There were posters for American bands and movies, jukeboxes, aging fruit machines and copulating clockwork rabbits in a glass case.

On a pillar, in a big silver frame, with a light over it, and a legend under it—"*New Art Work—Lester Jones*"—was "Lester's" picture. It had gained another title too. "Lick the Plate, Nigel," it was now called, for some unknown reason.

This was Gabriel's first exhibition: the first time art by him had been hung in public. But soon Gabriel began to feel unwell and not only because he suspected that "art" brought out the worst in people.

"Well hung, eh?" giggled Speedy. "It's a work of art!"

"A great work of great art," Dad repeated, putting his arm around Speedy.

"Of course everything in Splitz is art," Speedy went on. "And is original. But this is even more original than the other originals, which are also original. It's amazing. And here, with us, is Gabriel," said Speedy, turning instinctively to the camera that had been produced by the girl who'd greeted them at the door.

Gabriel, Speedy and the picture were photographed together. As Dad didn't want to be left out, a photograph of Dad, Gabriel and the picture soon followed.

Dad said, "You going to put one of these pictures up here, Speedy?"

"Maybe I will, if they turn out good."

"You've got lots of photographs. What you need in here," said Dad, "is a good old-fashioned painting of yourself, with you looking magnificent and handsome and in charge."

"That's a great idea. Anyone can have a photograph done.

But where would I get a portrait?" Speedy adopted a final pose. "Now—smile one more time, folks!"

Throughout this Gabriel remained quiet, though he kept glancing at the picture.

He knew Lester would feel betrayed by having a personal gift displayed like this without being asked. Not only that, the night Gabriel had crept into his mother's room, retrieved it from under the bed, and then stayed up, he hadn't copied the picture exactly how it was. He had, in fact, "improved" it a little here and there, adding other colors, lines and various experimental flourishes. Lester might have said that most art is theft; William Burroughs might have written that "all pictures are fakes"; but they can't have meant it literally. The picture might not be exceptionally valuable but Gabriel had forged Lester's signature—rather well, he thought. A career in crime would have been a possibility, if he weren't so sensitive. If the truth came out, Gabriel would be in serious trouble not only with Speedy, his parents and Lester, but with the police. It was Archie's fault. Archie had led him on. If Archie hadn't been dead, Gabriel would have killed him.

Speedy went on, "I can tell you boys—people are coming in just to look at this. Real Lester enthusiasts with seventies hair. The problem is, Lester was kinda anorexic in those days, and they don't eat as much as I would like. More good news—one of the national daily papers might run a story about it. What do you think about that, Gabriel?"

"Gabriel!" said Dad. "Pay attention!"

"It's lovely," said Gabriel. "Marvellously wonderful."

Speedy went on, "Maybe they'll use one of the pictures we just took! Your friends at school will be mightily impressed! Aren't you pleased?"

Gabriel put on his shades. "I'm delighted."

"But you're cool, too, eh?"

"That's right."

"Yes," said Dad. "He's bloody cool."

"That's good," said Speedy. "It's how a young boy should be."

"I'm not that young," said Gabriel.

"No, no, of course not," said Speedy. "At your age you seem to be all your ages at once."

"That's right," said Gabriel. "It is like that."

"See," said Dad. "I told you Speedy was cool."

"Yeah," said Gabriel.

Back at the table Gabriel took his father's beer and sipped it. Speedy beat him insistently on the shoulder. "What do you think?"

"I'm very proud . . . of Lester," said Gabriel.

"Good, good," said Speedy. "Me too."

"Really, aren't you pleased?" asked Dad, trying to peer into Gabriel's glasses. "Everyone can see it now. It's democratic, right? And of course you can come and sit here and look at it whenever you like."

Gabriel asked Speedy, "Does Lester come here?"

"Oh yes, yes. He has been here, a few years back," said Speedy. "But I can't say he's a regular visitor, no." Gabriel sighed in relief. "But his friends come in. Like guide dogs, they keep an eye on things for him."

When at last, having ordered more drinks and food for Dad, and having spotted a TV presenter and a footballer at the entrance—though he was only a mid-fielder from the First Division—Speedy sped away. Gabriel tried to breathe more easily and take in the enormity of what had happened.

"You're quiet," said Dad. He was eating and drinking rapidly. "It's free." His cheeks were bulging.

"So? I'm thinking."

"Thank God for that. Your eye is twitching too. Do you know why?"

"Did you get a good price for the picture?"

"Sorry?"

"Did you, Dad?"

Gabriel saw his father's embarrassment. It hadn't been his intention to make his father feel bad. In fact Gabriel had been thinking that, despite everything, they all had what they wanted. Gabriel's mother had a picture by "Lester"; Speedy had a picture by "Lester"; Gabriel had the original in his room; and his father had some money.

"Not what I'd expected or hoped for," said Dad. "Speedy's shrewd. But what I got was better than nothing." Dad leaned across the table. "Sometimes living is more important than a few squiggles on a piece of paper."

"What will you do with the money? Get a flat in a mansion block?"

"A flat? A toilet, maybe. Or a window—without curtains!" His father laughed without humor.

"How long will the money last?"

"I've saved some for you, but otherwise it's nearly gone."

"On what?"

"Food, booze, rent and my debts, which are considerable. It's expensive out there. Mum always looked after the money. I had no idea what things cost."

"What will you do now?"

"I've borrowed more from the man downstairs. I had no choice. What else could I do?"

"How will you pay it back?"

"Really, I don't know," said Dad. "I had a bad argument with the landlord and he's told me to get out. I'm going to end up sleeping on the street. Look out for me at tube stations singing 'The Streets of London.' I'm afraid it might be the end of the road for me, Angel."

"Can't you stay with a mate?"

"For how long? Anyway the wives won't have me there."

"Why?"

"They say I'm a bad influence! Me! I've known those people for years—and they won't have me in the house! I tell you, kid, after a time, all a man wants is a little peace. Unfortunately, the calmest state of mind is happiness, and I'm a long, long way from that. Anyhow, I don't think I should burden you with this. Is she seeing anyone else?"

"I don't think so."

"She is, then."

"I didn't say that."

"You did. Is it that guy who was there the time I phoned? How often does she see him? Is he sleeping on my side of the bed with his head on my pillow?" Dad sighed. "Sorry to ask you this stuff. How would you know anyway?"

"I do know. I was under the bed."

"You were what?"

"Only joking, Dad."

Dad leaned forward, screwing up his face and squeezing his hands between his knees.

"You're making me crazy, Gabriel. Jesus! Will he move into my house? Will he take you, too? Christ, Gabriel, really I don't want to know. I'm being wiped out. All the people closest to me have let me down. I've lost everything. Cheerio."

"No, Dad."

"I hope he's looking after her. How old is he? Younger than me, and very active, too, I expect. She could be a beautiful lover, your mother. She'd do things to my ears, to my face, and the rest of me, for that matter, that would make your hair stand on end. That was when she bothered. But she stopped. It all stopped, and she started wearing those big grey knickers. That's the thing about love, it's a fire you have to feed, otherwise it goes out. This one, I'm afraid, is going out."

Gabriel said nothing.

Dad said, "What a mess."

His father turned his face away. Gabriel handed him a napkin. Dad blew his nose.

"Oh, Dad," said Gabriel.

"If you're going to go on about how I've crooked you—"

"But I'm not!"

"Yes you are! We can always get the picture back."

"What? How?" said Gabriel.

"Speedy said I could buy it back from him if I decided to change my mind."

"But we'll never get the money."

"We'd have to pay a bit more for it, too. Speedy's got a good nose for a number of things and profit is the first of them. I've still got some of my instruments in a mate's garage. I'll sell them. The bike, too."

"You need those things."

"But why, Gabriel, would we need the picture back? Even if I had the 'Mona Lisa' in the living room I wouldn't look at it all the time. The thing is, I don't know how much more of this I can take."

"More of what?"

"These blows to the heart. Gabriel, I'm losing hope. I need all my resources but I've never had less. Can you believe it, you're all I've got! I've always liked being with you too much. Why didn't I achieve anything with my life? I'd rather spend the day hanging out with you than working or hustling. If anyone asked me who my best friend was, I'd say you. Christ Almighty!"

"Dad, Dad—don't cry!"

"Let's get out of here. I don't want Speedy to see me blubbing."

"Right."

When they'd finished their food and were about to leave, Speedy came over to the table.

"I forgot to tell you," said Speedy. "There's this kid—the son of a personal friend of mine, the movie producer Jake Ambler. The guy who made *Timeless Saturday* and all that other great stuff."

"We know, we know," said Dad, wiping his eyes. "*Timeless*

Saturday is one of the greats. The way he edited that middle section and uses music to—"

"Jake loves the waffles in here. Have you had them? I'm not allowed to trust him with the ice cream—it's like cocaine to him. His kid is in a group, they've even got the possibility of a record contract and all that, but he can't play that well. He's stuck at a certain point. You know what I'm talking about, Rex. Jake and I were gossiping about Lester and your name came up. Jake saw you play a lot of times. I told him, 'Rex has been coming in here on business. Rex helped me start up at the beginning.'"

"You told him that?"

"Yeah. You said to me, years ago, 'You'll be more successful than any of us.'"

"That's right. And you are, man. You're one of the great . . . great multimillionaires of our time."

"Sweet of you, Rex."

"Why is it, d'you think, that almost everyone I know has got more money than me?"

"Maybe it's connected to the fact you don't work, Rex." Gabriel tried to stop himself laughing. Speedy went on, "Listen, Jake knows, without me telling him, that you're one of the best. I said you wouldn't mind going over to his place and showing the kid a few of those chunky rock 'n' roll chords—"

"I don't know about showing him some chords," said Dad. "As it is, people don't use instruments any more. It's all computers. Besides, I'm pretty busy at the moment."

"Wow. What are you doing?" said Speedy. He looked at Gabriel and crinkled his nose. "I prefer gossip to food."

Dad said, "There's this opera about—"

Gabriel squeezed his father's arm. "Dad, listen to him. It's a stroke. Please carry on, Mr. Speedy."

"Jake will pay well, there's no problem with that. The more he pays, the more he'll appreciate it. Isn't that always the way?" Speedy pursed his lips. "You'll be able to upgrade your bike."

"Bike?"

"I've seen you on it."

Dad got up. "Jake can blow it out his arse. We're not so desperate that we're going to start working for a living."

"We are," said Gabriel. "Aren't we?"

Dad stumbled towards the door.

"Dear, oh dear," said Speedy. "Who's pissed on his rose bush?"

"He's broken up with Mum."

Speedy nodded. "I see."

Gabriel said, "Please, Mr. Speedy, what's the number of this boy who needs the talent lessons?"

"I'll give it to you." Speedy moved closer to him. "But only if you promise something. I want you to come and see me."

"Me? What for?"

"Oh I like a direct boy. Gabriel, we can talk. I know what it's like."

"You know what what's like?"

"The turbulence that young guys are prone to."

"I see. Thanks." Speedy's pen was poised. Gabriel said, "I will come by."

"So you should. You know where I am. I can guarantee that it'll be worth it. Here." He wrote down the name and phone number on a piece of paper.

"Thanks again."

"The pleasure is mine," Speedy said. "You have a very pleasant manner. See you soon."

Speedy was smiling at him. Gabriel wondered if he'd smile if he knew the true history of "Lester's" picture. Luckily Gabriel wouldn't have to see him again.

Nine

Sitting in the entrance hall of Dad's house, surrounded by several men and clicking a long string of beads, was the man with curly slippers who had lent Dad money. Once more he nodded at Gabriel and his father.

Dad had bought several cans of beer on the way home. Before he could go upstairs and drink in earnest, Gabriel led him to the telephone in the corridor and told him to ring the film producer.

"Now?" his father kept saying. "Why now?"

"Why not now?"

"He's an important man. He'll be in Los Angeles with movie stars, or somewhere not anywhere near us."

Gabriel extracted the piece of paper from his pocket, dialed the number and handed his father the receiver.

"Big Picture Films. Hello, hello—" the voice on the other end was saying.

"Say who you are," urged Gabriel.

"Rex Bunch speaking." Dad whispered, "For better or worse."

"Who?" said the voice. "Can you tell me what it is about?"

"Guitars. And chords."

"Sorry?"

To Dad's surprise and disappointment, he was, eventually, connected to Jake, who said, "I'm so pleased you rang. Rex—"

Pushing his ear close to the phone, Gabriel could hear how keen Jake was. He was saying that years ago he had seen Dad on stage with Lester.

"That was my sound," Dad interjected. "We did that together, Lester and I!"

"Incredible! I still play those records in my cars. Please, could you come over this afternoon and help my boy out?"

"I would," said Dad. "But the thing is—" He started to explain he was working on his opera about rebirth.

"Oh," said Jake. "Thanks anyway for ringing. Are you absolutely certain—?"

Gabriel grasped his father's wrist and twisted it until he agreed to give a first lesson later that day.

Gabriel was pleased: it meant he could accompany his father to ensure that he didn't deliberately make a mess of things.

"Why are you bothering me with all this?" Dad was trying to pull himself upstairs. Gabriel had begun to realize how drunk Dad had got at Speedy's. "I need to rest while I've still got a bed."

"Rest? You haven't done anything!"

"Seeing Speedy makes me feel weak."

Dad might have been feeling weak but next to the bed was an orange box on which were his rolling papers, glasses and notebooks. Dad kicked the box across the room.

"Fuck everything—I'm not going anywhere!" He lay down on the bed and closed his eyes. The beer cans, one of them open, were on the floor where he could reach them. "Goodnight. I'm sorry for everything, kiddo. Turn out the lights. Forgive me and kiss me."

"I'm not kissing an arse like you."

"Your own father's a bloody arse now?"

"You are," said Gabriel.

His father said, "I wish I had the strength to thump you! Now piss off and don't bang the door—it might fall off its hinges and I'll have to pay for it!" Dad laughed to himself and sang, "Valhalla, I am coming!"

Soon his father was snoring. Gabriel knew he wouldn't wake up in time to give his lesson.

Gabriel left him and went downstairs. Every step he took away from the house made him feel bad. Archie was restless; he didn't say anything, but he wasn't happy. Gabriel wanted to go to Mum's bar and ask her to try and get Dad out of bed. But she wouldn't be prepared to do it; she'd given up on him. Everyone had, now.

Gabriel waited at the bus stop. He'd count to a hundred. If the bus didn't come, he'd go back. He started to count; he lost his place and started again. He decided to do it backwards. The bus came. He got on and started up to the top deck. He couldn't just go home and think about something else.

As the bus was gathering speed, Gabriel jumped down the stairs and threw himself off, scuffing his knee and grazing his hands. He couldn't forget how, months ago, his father had rescued him from the "drum."

He went back and kneeled beside his father's bed, talking into Dad's face. He looked so relaxed for the first time in months that Gabriel didn't like to disturb him.

"Wake up," he said. "You can sleep later."

Dad stroked Gabriel's face. "It *is* later. I was dreaming that I was at an airport but they wouldn't let me on the planes and I was crying. Gabriel, if I'm asleep, at least I'm not feeling wretched."

"You know what Mum says?"

"Who cares? What does she think?"

"She says you're useless, a waster, lazy and slow. What kind of future will I have watching you sit on your arse and drink all day?"

"She said that?"

"She says I can't see you if you're going to depress me with your hopelessness and self-pity."

"It's what she would say. Everyone says it."

"I don't. If I don't have a proper dad, who will look after me? I still need you, Dad. I want you to do this thing for me."

"What thing?"

"Go to Jake's as arranged."

"I'm not in the mood, Gabriel. You know how I'm feeling."

"You'll cheer up when you're there. We need the money. Dad—"

"Why are you getting upset?"

"Your stupidity makes me upset! Give me a drink!"

"Hey, put that down right now! It's the strongest there is— you'll puke! Take it easy, little guy. I don't like to see you like this!"

Gabriel said, "I'm not leaving until you get up!"

"Right, right," said Dad. "I see. Please put the beer down."

"Get up, then!"

"Wait . . ."

Gabriel watched Dad slowly begin to move, as if he were discovering for the first time that he had a body. When Dad got to his feet Gabriel gave a little cheer.

Dad began to throw his clothes about.

"Boy, help me find my razor. I'm not going to cut my throat, though I've been considering it for the last few days. I'll shave. You're the only person I'd do this for. I wouldn't take orders from anyone else!"

Gabriel went up the hall to borrow an iron; together they

pressed Dad's white shirt, holding it up and turning the sleeves and tail here and there, like explorers who'd come across an object they'd never seen before.

"Better clean your teeth," said Gabriel.

"I smell now?"

"You've been drinking. And you smell of fish."

"This is rock 'n' roll."

"Not today, I'm afraid."

Dad asked, "How are you feeling now?"

"A bit better."

He made his father leave with plenty of time to spare, as Dad used to do with Gabriel himself, before school. This time, as Dad had his guitar and it wasn't far, they walked.

Dad moaned all the way like a morose teenager. "Why would anyone want to be taught to play the guitar? Play is playing. I learned from records."

"Take it easy with the philosophy," suggested Gabriel. "Hold the five-pound notes at the front of your mind."

"Money's not everything. It's just that I've been feeling a bit low these days—"

"You'll be telling me you've got a tummy ache."

"People only ever learn what they want to learn, just as you can't force them to eat."

Gabriel said quickly, "Maybe you can introduce them to food they've never had before."

This encouraged Dad, but Gabriel could see that his pride was bruised by the possibility of this job. He wanted to see himself as a working musician. Teaching was the death of invention and certainly of pop glamour. Somehow Dad had to be convinced that it was possible to instruct as well as to play and perform.

The two of them stood outside a big house with iron gates, like menials beyond a medieval castle. Gabriel held the guitar in one hand and his father's hand in the other, for fear he would slip away.

"Christ," said his father. "You wouldn't catch Jimmy Page doing this."

"You're not—" Gabriel stopped himself.

Dad didn't hear; he was looking up at the house. "Look how posh they are—I expect they have their pajamas dry-cleaned."

The gates opened automatically as a robotic voice on an invisible intercom said, "Visitors, please enter now."

In the entrance hall they passed a line of oriental staff in white uniforms with shiny buttons in which Gabriel could see a fish-eyed distortion of his father's worried face. Being given instructions by a man in a black suit, the servants had their hands crossed in front of them, as if they were naked and didn't want their intimate parts exposed.

Gabriel gazed up at a wide curved staircase and imagined a singing diva in a trailing white dress coming down it. Around them it was as busy as backstage at the opera. The staff and producer's assistants hurried between wide rooms containing gilt and velvet furniture, overhung by intricate chandeliers. There must have been a fancy-dress party going on, as little girls dressed as princesses and boys in pirate costumes were ushered about by nannies.

The kid himself, Carlo, was about two years older than Gabriel. He was brought to them—or rather, almost dragged across—by a woman whom Gabriel guessed, from his knowledge of Gothic tales, to be the housekeeper. She rid herself of the boy—if he'd been a thing, she'd have flung him down, and if she'd been allowed, no doubt she'd have stamped on the thing, too—and disappeared with some relief and haste.

Carlo was bony and crop-haired, with a criminal grimace, wearing a Chelsea shirt over torn baggy jeans; his feet were bare and dirty.

"How are you today?" said Dad. "This is my boy, Gabriel. He goes to Chapman High. D'you know it?"

"Na."

"Where do you go?"

"Nowhere . . . if I can 'elp it."

"What, if anything, do you want?"

There was a silence. At last the boy said, "A tattoo."

"Right. Where?"

"On me bollocks and round me arse."

"I see," said Dad. "Interesting. Not a lot of people are going to enjoy it there."

"'Ow d'you know?"

"I don't, really. I don't do tattoos, but I can play guitar a bit."

Carlo had undoubtedly been well brought up but was unable to put one word beside another without grunting and snarling between them, and he suffered to look anyone in the eye.

"This way, I suppose," Carlo mumbled, after the three of them had been shuffling about. To Gabriel he said, "You coming an' all?"

"D'you want me to?" murmured Gabriel.

"It's up to you."

Carlo started up the stairs.

"Public school education," muttered Dad to Gabriel. "One of those schools for talented parents. At least the working class have manners. A Chelsea supporter too, of all things. I'm off."

"Wait." Gabriel held on to his father with both hands. "Come on. At least let's have a look."

Gabriel and his father followed Carlo up the staircase to a vast living room with a view of the Thames. There the boy stood with his back to a bookcase and stuck his arse out. At this the bookcase smoothly swung open into his part of the house.

Behind the bookcase Carlo had two or three teenage rooms, including a kitchen and bathroom. It was a rich squalor the boy had made for himself; among the mounds of clothes, magazines and CDs, Gabriel noticed computers, a drum kit, various guitars and, in the distance, a shiny grand piano. There was a basket containing dozens of pairs of sunglasses.

Carlo sat in a window, turned away from them, craning his neck as if he urgently needed to inspect Battersea.

"D'you want to play something . . . on the guitar?" said Dad. "Or do you want to do something else? I don't give a—" Gabriel gave his father a scalding look. "I don't really mind. It's your time." He was looking at the boy in annoyance and sat there with his coat buttoned up.

Carlo shrugged.

Gabriel was becoming apprehensive, wondering how long Dad would remain patient. If his father walked out, it would be the end, his teaching career terminated within twenty minutes. Gabriel had no idea what sort of job his father would do, anyway. It was true that Dad could play; he could also scratch his backside and fiddle in his ear at the same time: it didn't follow that he could instruct anyone in ambidexterity.

Carlo did, at last, decide to say something. "You know what you are?"

"What am I?" said Dad. "Been trying to find out for years."

"You're a . . . You're a . . ."

Dad said, "I'm waiting here, but you haven't got the balls to say it, little big guy. If you do it'll be annoying, but at least it will be rock 'n' roll."

"Wanker," said Carlo.

Gabriel was holding his breath. Dad winked at him.

Dad unzipped his acoustic guitar and lightly strummed what sounded like a pleasant folksy tune.

"What d'you think?" said Dad.

"Wanker scumbag," the boy repeated.

"Hey!" said Gabriel.

"What is it?" said the boy. "Something to say?"

"Dad—" said Gabriel.

"Dad . . ." imitated the boy. "Is that your daddy-poo?"

Gabriel's eyes fixed on a Coke bottle on the table. He intertwined his fingers and clicked them. Carlo was sneering. Gabriel started to get up, breathing hard. Carlo got to his feet, too. The boys moved towards one another until they were face to face.

"Yeah?" said Carlo.

"Yeah?" said Gabriel.

Dad said, "Sit down, Gabriel. You, too, Carlo. Sit down! Now, cool it, people. Cool it! Jesus, I'm sweating all over the place now. Good."

When the boys had regained their places Dad lay the guitar down and looked about enquiringly with meanly flashing eyes. Things weren't right for him and they weren't getting better. "Funky Fingers" had, after all, played with Lester Jones at Madison Square Garden. For three nights they'd ripped the place apart. No one, apart from the Stones, had been that good.

Dad removed his coat, tossed the Coke bottle across the room into a bin, and picked up one of the kid's electric guitars.

"Carlo, tell me something," he said. "What d'you call this?"

"Some people call it a guitar."

Dad plugged it in and stroked the strings. A tinny noise emerged.

"What the hell's that—a weeping mouse?" said Dad.

The boy shrugged. "Call it what you like, man, I don't give a monkey's."

Dad got to his feet.

Gabriel's father, in most ways by now a respectable middle-aged father, stepped back and took a kick at one of the expensive speakers, his boot breaking through the front of it. They would, surely, be ejected now.

Dad, grinning with satisfaction at this memory of rock 'n' roll, turned the volume up to "unbearable," and scythed across the strings. A blaze of noise and jagged feedback penetrated the three of them like fiery arrows. The boy, who had sat up at Dad's attitude, seemed to stagger under the noise.

"Why whisper?" said Dad. "This is the devil's music. Or it is when it's done properly."

It was a blues number, one of Gabriel's favorites, "Mean Old World." Dad was banging his foot and singing, though they couldn't hear a word but saw only his opened mouth so that he resembled one of Bacon's screaming popes.

Crouched over as if to avoid a hail of bullets, two of the staff ran into the room with their hands over their ears. They struggled to close the windows, and, to make absolutely sure, dragged the curtains across. Then they scurried out across the vibrating floor, whimpering.

The boy grabbed a guitar, turned up the volume, stabbed and twisted his foot in the front of another speaker—at least he had learned that aggression was imperative for a vivid performance—and started to play, pursuing his teacher into the distance.

The boy managed a decent bluesy sound and when Dad paused, keeping the rhythm, the boy took over.

As his father worked, letting Carlo play along with him, not forcing him to do anything, and the boy began to see he could do it, Gabriel could settle down to biting his fingernails and chewing his cheek. Gabriel had never worried about anything as much as Lester's picture, though perhaps he didn't have to take any action at the moment. Lester might not become aware of the picture's whereabouts for a long time, and even then, might not realize that the picture was a forgery. Maybe, in the future, he could write Lester a letter. Dad had the address.

When Gabriel and his father got up to leave he noticed, to his surprise, Carlo's father standing in the door. The film producer was small, jovial and bald, in a good suit without a tie. With the top button of his shirt done up and his Adam's apple seeming to still bob with the beat, his head looked constrained, like a boil about to burst.

Dad had told Gabriel that Jake Ambler was so busy he would invite people who sought meetings with him to sit in his car on the way to the airport, or even to walk around the building with him, as he ate his lunch or went to the toilet.

"Thank you so much," Jake said, following Dad and Gabriel down the stairs, tearing notes from an impressive wad and pushing them into Dad's hand. "You deserve this. I enjoyed that so much I felt like getting my leather trousers let out."

Dad turned and looked at him, nervous of any condescension. There was none; the man was looking at him gratefully.

Jake said quietly, "Carlo didn't say anything offensive did he?"

"Like what?"

"Well . . . you know . . . that you were a self-abuser."

"No," said Dad. "He didn't mention anything like that."

"I'm relieved. I can't seem to find the right tone with him. He's my only son, Rex. It's terrible: the boy has strange turns."

"He does?"

"When he goes to sleep he thinks flies walk over his body. He thinks policemen are watching him. We sent him to that therapist that people have started seeing, the one who wrote the book, Deedee Osgood. Have you met her yet? Carlo seemed to get very attached to her, but it didn't cure him. He won't learn anything but the one thing he's interested in is music. He's either playing or listening, all the time. Music can make people feel better, can't it?"

"It's always had that effect on me."

"Please, will you try it with him, then?"

"Try what?"

"Teaching him stuff—anything that you know—through music."

"I'd like to be of help, Jake. I'm flattered and all that. But I've never done it before. I'm not qualified."

"I don't care about that. The boy has worshipped Lester for years. He wouldn't show it, but he was very excited when he heard you were coming. He'll see you, I know he will. Please, give it a go—just for a while. If it doesn't work out, nothing will have been lost."

"It's strange," said Dad. "I know how the boy feels. For

years I could hardly speak. I didn't like other people standing too close to me. Music was the only thing that went into my head. Let me think."

Dad walked away and seemed to be thinking a bit, though mostly he was fiddling with his hair. Jake and Gabriel watched him. At last Dad agreed to come by every other day to give the boy lessons.

"I don't know what I'll do," said Dad. "But I don't mind telling him some of the things I know."

"I'm delighted!" said Jake, shaking his hand. "You must come round for dinner. I'll get some people in that you might like. Can my driver drop you anywhere? He's at your disposal—both of you."

"No thanks," said Rex, before Gabriel could say anything. "We like the street. We're used to having our feet on the ground."

When Gabriel and Dad were turning the corner, Carlo ran up behind them and shoved tapes of his father's films into Gabriel's arms and whispered, "He's all right, your father."

"Thanks for saying that," said Gabriel.

Dad lit a joint and they walked away through the cold air.

"I'm surprised you didn't smack that kid across the room," said Gabriel. "I was getting ready to."

"I noticed. You could have easily taken the skinny little bastard. But it wouldn't have created a good impression with his old man if you'd put that bottle through his head."

"No."

"He didn't bother me one bit," said Dad. "I'm glad we went. But I am exhausted. I couldn't go through all that again, even if they paid me. I'll ring and say I'm emigrating to Africa."

"No you won't. Surely we didn't go through all that for nothing?"

Dad said, "Do you know why people become teachers?"

"In my experience, because they like being listened to."

"That's a good reason for being one, then, if you have something to say." Dad counted the money three times and whistled. "To think—all these years I've been passing on my opinions in pubs for nothing!" He said quickly, "You know, when that kid started cursing me, I remembered that my mum was a primary school teacher. I'd sort of forgotten that. She was devoted to it, too. She was hardly at home and when she was there she was preparing for the next day. We'd run into her adoring ex-pupils all over the place, waving and saying hello. Whenever I went to the school there was always a kid holding on to her. I hated that."

"Why?"

"I wanted her to be only mine. But she could do this remarkable thing—she knew how to make kids feel she was on their side."

"How did she do that?"

"By being really on their side. By disliking authority." Dad was sobbing. "I haven't thought about her for a long time. Can you believe it—I'm talking about more than forty years ago. Maybe in forty years, long after I'm dead, you'll remember this moment. I often think about how you'll remember me. Maybe you'll put me in a film or something. Who could play me, d'you think? How about Robert De Niro?"

"Won't you be around when I'm old? I want you here for ever."

"Yeah, I know. I'll try and last as long as I can, pal. But I'll be dead before you, I hope. You'll have a son and you can tell him all about our adventures together. The stupid things I used to do . . . and how I sold your picture . . . and how I—"

"Yes."

"Whatever. Shall we go and eat? Things are looking up a little. We should celebrate, eh?"

He took Gabriel to a good Italian place where they filled themselves up with pasta and ice cream.

It had been a busy day but to Gabriel's surprise Dad wasn't

depleted. The teaching had reinvigorated him. Gabriel himself had even managed to temporarily forget about the picture. It was, of course, hanging in Splitz, but Lester didn't go there.

Later, at the top of their road, Gabriel said, "Mum will be pleased."

"About what?"

"The teaching job."

"Will you tell her?"

"It would be better coming from you," said Gabriel. "She keeps saying to me that there's something important she wants to talk about, but she never gets round to it."

"D'you know what it is?"

Gabriel shrugged. "The future, I expect. Dad, why don't you come round?"

"I've thought about it. But I can't go into the house . . . it's heartbreaking. Even walking about this area makes me feel sick."

"Go to the bar where she works."

"Do you think she'd been happy to talk to me? She's falling in love with someone else."

"It doesn't matter. I've never met a bigger idiot than that guy. She's only trying to make you jealous."

"Yeah? I'll think about it. My problem is, I don't really want anyone else. But she's been rather hard on me."

"It's for your own good."

"Thank you, Gabriel, but I don't feel improved by it yet."

Gabriel kissed his father.

"See you soon, Dad."

"See you."

Ten

One Sunday morning a couple of weeks later, when at last he got up, Gabriel found Hannah had bared her thick arms and donned rubber gloves, covered her head with a ragged tea towel, and put on a pair of his father's old shoes, without laces. Gabriel wondered if she were about to tackle a pile of nuclear waste, but saw she was intending to clean the living room. Mum had had people round: the sour air was thick and muzzy, the ashtrays full, the chairs scattered, and on the table were beer and wine bottles, crisp packets and half-eaten sandwiches.

Afraid Hannah might hand him a mop or duster, he skipped through into the kitchen. To his surprise he found his mother listening to a waltz on the radio and cooking him a fried breakfast.

"Hi, Angel. It's a lovely day. How about going to Kew Gardens?"

The suggestion startled him; he quite liked Hannah now, but he didn't want to spend the day in a hothouse with her.

He said, "I'm going swimming with a mate."

Mum said, "I thought it would be nice for us to go out."

Gabriel and his parents often used to go to Kew Gardens on Sundays. They had taken many photographs there. It must have been two years since they'd last visited.

He said, "You and me?"

"Yes."

"No George?"

"There is something I've been meaning to talk to you about."

He said, "No Hannah, either."

His mother put her finger to her lips. "I wouldn't do that to you. Anyhow, she's decided to do some work."

During breakfast he watched his mother skeptically. He wasn't convinced she was actually going to walk out of the door with him.

They did, at last, say goodbye to Hannah. Gabriel was even more surprised when, taking his hand, his mother said they'd be going to Kew on the tube. He didn't know how long it had been since she'd got on a train, but she had stopped traveling on the underground for a variety of sensible reasons: it was beneath the earth and the experience resembled being buried alive; it was polluted—killer gases and toxic odors could poison you; and only murderers and lunatics traveled on the District Line.

He was apprehensive walking beside her on the way to the station; he could feel how afraid she was. Once they were on the train—while she read the papers with perhaps more interest than the *Sunday Times* merited—she glanced about nervously, but managed to keep her fear down. What she used to consider a boiling hell was an almost empty carriage rattling over the wide, beautiful, dirty Thames on a Sunday morning.

When they got off she sighed in relief.

"Brave, eh?" she said.

"Well done, Mum."

"It'll be an airplane next. It's too late to be scared of everything." She looked him over. "Pull that hood down—"

"Mum—"

"Pull it down! Out here people will think you're a drug dealer!"

For them, cool clean Kew was the countryside; it was a place to dream in.

Mum talked thoughtfully of how the English loved gardens and their houses, and how tedious she used to find it. But when she visited a middle-class area like Kew it cleared her mind and she could see she wanted more than the weed-infested patch of concrete containing rotting bookshelves and a burnt saucepan that they had at the back of the house. When she started to earn more money they would move.

"We'll get a proper garden," she said. "It won't be big—just the right size for the two of us to sit out."

They would be there, she added, until he went to university.

She said, "When I was in my twenties, living off the King's Road and knowing fashionable people, I was quite a strange girl, lonely and . . ." She searched for the word. "Extreme. I haven't made the most of myself. In those days I would calm myself by thinking of being sixty. A sprightly woman I'd be, always well dressed but with weak knees, bent toes and bright eyes, reading French novels and listening to *The Seven Deadly Sins*. You can bring me flowers and books. You will come, won't you, even though you'll have better things to do? Perhaps you will bring your own children."

"Why would I not come?" he said.

"Children have to fall out of love with their parents. It's a terrible divorce. My own parents have nothing to say to me, as you've probably noticed. I left them at fifteen. And yet I will want you to come to me. What's wrong?"

"It seems funny," he said. "Waiting until you're sixty before you do what you want to do. Why can't you do it now?"

"It's a good question. I wish I knew."

As she talked, Gabriel found it odd, their being together alone. Usually, when they went on an outing, his father would be chattering, drawing attention to himself, making jokes, singing.

Neither mother nor son mentioned him, but Gabriel kept thinking of whether his father was still in his bed in his room, or if he had enough money to go out for breakfast. Maybe he had gone for a walk? Gabriel couldn't get rid of the idea that Dad would decide to come to Kew Gardens. He would step out from behind the pagoda and the three of them would link arms and walk together.

On the way back to the tube they passed a little bookshop.

"Would you like to go in?"

"Yes. I might get something to read," Gabriel said, hopefully.

"You can have whatever you want."

"Anything?"

"Choose what takes your fancy—I'll get it for you. It might surprise you, but I have been earning some money out there! Your father hasn't been sending us any money, even though I've written to ask him. There's the bills and mortgage on the house, and you're expensive to run."

He took a long time but she waited, looking around herself, mostly at the self-help section. As Zak had pointed out, it was when you heard the word "healing" that you knew there'd be parent trouble ahead. There'd be therapy or worse, hypnotism or other forms of weird religion. Numerous members of Zak's clan were walking about with their arms extended in front of them, and their eyes closed, "realigning" their lives.

Among the limited selection of art books, Gabriel found a book of portraits. Mum commended his choice; it surprised her how few contemporary artists were interested in the human face and in what people were really like. It was a subject that rock 'n' roll couldn't explore.

Carrying his new book, they went to a café a few doors down and had pizza. He wondered if he could have what he'd called, as a child, a "curly one"—a knickerbocker glory. She said yes and ordered a spoon for herself.

He noticed she was looking around. "Don't they serve beer here?"

"It's a café. Why do you want beer?"

She passed her hand over her face. "You make things hard for me."

"Thought it might be my fault."

"No, Gabriel."

He was eating intently; it was a while before he realized she was watching him.

"You used to be such a noisy little boy."

"Did I?"

"Or perhaps I found you difficult. I was suffering, for other reasons. You've become quite thoughtful. What were you thinking about just then?"

He replied, "Whether Dad prefers chocolate or coffee ice cream." Gabriel, Dad and Mum had kept a row of ice creams in the freezer and often enthusiastically debated the subject of their favorite flavor. "Chocolate, I think. Dad could be eating one now . . . at the same time as us."

She handed Gabriel her handkerchief. "Wipe your face, big boy. You miss him? He's not dead, Gabriel darling."

"No, he's living in a bedsit."

"It's not a catastrophe. He was unhappy, your father. He didn't even know it. Now he's been made to see its effect on others."

"You've done him a favor?" He whispered, "It'd be the first."

"Don't mumble. I knew there was something wrong when he stopped hating everything. He didn't complain about what he watched, ate or heard. He was moving far away from us—or me, at least. Sorry for leaving you with Hannah—as my mother used to say, she's got a face like a bag of hammers. But I had to get things going. The petrification—that means things staying the same—was killing me. I have my faults, but I haven't given up." She stood up, raised her arms and sat down. "Look at me, don't I have some energy? Even more now, since he's gone."

"Dad could be at work right now."

"Work? Gabriel, apart from everything else, it's Sunday."

"He's started to teach."

"Teach, did you say? What sort of teaching is it?"

When he saw she wasn't about to be sarcastic, Gabriel explained that Dad had been teaching guitar to a boy, who had, in turn, recommended him to another, less spiky, kid whom Dad had enjoyed being with. He had signed up to teach them both for a few weeks. "When I'm teaching," Dad had said, "it's strange, but I don't get stuck in one particular state of mind. It shakes me up good."

Gabriel could see that Mum wanted to talk about Rex, his father—to someone who knew him, who would understand. At the same time, she knew she couldn't say all she felt.

"Gabriel, I can imagine him teaching. He's bad-tempered and testy, your father, and he'd be surprised that his pupils don't know everything already. But he understands music. In certain moods, he likes to . . . lecture. I haven't talked to Lester for years, but he was always incredibly alive and energetic. Maybe he's inspired Dad. It's obviously done him good."

In this was some surprising generosity.

Gabriel said, "Grandma—Dad's mum—was a teacher."

Her face brightened. "Oh yes, that's right. She'd take you to the library."

"Didn't she teach me to read?"

"Yes, with my help."

Gabriel said, "Dad and I did stuff together, but you were always shouting at him about the sticky patch on the living room floor."

"Weeks it was there, that sticky patch. I kept getting glued to the floor. I thought I'd never move again."

"He got discouraged." Gabriel had read somewhere that people say this when they are angry: "Anyhow, I can't forgive you for it."

She was shocked. "What made you say that?"

"Archie."

"Archie? You're talking about your brother now?"

"Yes."

She said, "My son's dead. It nearly drove me mad. I was on medication for a long time—"

"Archie's almost dead."

"Almost! What are you saying? Gabriel—"

"He's a part of me. He talks to me."

"Archie talks to you? What does he say?"

"He gives me advice."

"That's odd, seeing as he never became much of a talker. Now you're saying he's having conversations. Gabriel you had better watch out—the psychiatrists'll be round tapping your knees with hammers and asking you your own name. Does your father know anything about this?"

"No."

"I should talk to him about it. Except we're not talking."

"Why don't you?"

"I might have to. I can't believe it. Christ Almighty, what's happened to you? What a strange little boy you are!"

"I'm not little any more! You should open your eyes!"

Mum was looking at Gabriel in puzzlement. She snatched back her handkerchief. She said, "Oh, you don't understand how people can make one another crazy. Gabriel, don't you dare try to make me feel guilty. Parents always feel they fail. It's a losing game, parenthood. I'm a woman on her own, without a useful husband, trying to make a living for us both! A single mother!"

"Single mother," he imitated her.

"What do you expect me to do? It's no party at work!"

"You have plenty of parties!"

"And why not?" She shook herself, flinging off agitation like rainwater. "I've got to tell you—I've been offered a new job . . ."

"Really?"

"By a man called Speedy."

"Speedy?"

"Yes. What's it to you?"

He said, "Strange name."

"He's always in a hurry. I ran into him at a party in the Portobello Road a little while ago. We were friends in the old days. He had a villa near Marrakech where we all stayed. He always wore shiny shirts. Many of the people are dead now, or mad, or have moved to Wales. But Speedy owns hamburger places full of rock and pop stuff. He knows my situation with Dad, and he's sympathetic. I think he's going to employ me. At first I'll do some waitressing. Then he'll promote me. I'm pretty sure I'll get to manage one of the places. It's a good start. What do you say?"

"Er . . . I'll have to think about it."

"Why? It's not a philosophical problem! Aren't you pleased at my new job?"

He nodded and said, "Have you been to this hamburger place?"

"Oh, I used to go there, only for parties, not for the food, of course. I'd rather eat my feet. But I told you," she said impatiently. "Don't you listen? I ran into Speedy at a party. I was thinking, too," she went on, "that we should show Lester's picture to Speedy."

"Lester's picture?"

"Yes."

"What for?"

"He might be interested. Anyway, even if we don't do that, I think we should have it framed. I'm going to see to that next week. Before I start the new job, I thought we might go to Italy."

"To see George's castle?"

"Yes."

Gabriel said, "I don't like castles."

"Oh, don't you?"

"They're too drafty. I want to work on my film."

"Good. You can do it there. Oh, Gabriel, it'll be wonderful for us to have some sun and sea. It's been so long since things were good!"

"I can only work in London. It's the environment in which I feel most comfortable."

"Oh really? You're a cussed devil. You'll have to stay with Hannah, then."

"I'll stay with Dad, I think."

She snorted, "He won't be able to look after you."

"I can look after myself."

"I'm not sure that you can, yet," she said. "But soon you'll have to. I haven't been with you much lately, but I've been thinking a lot about your future."

"Have you?" he said enthusiastically.

"I know you love movies and directors and actors and all that—"

"Yes, yes—I've been having so many ideas recently. Have you ever written down your dreams? Maybe one day there'll be a method for photographing them!"

"That'll be interesting," she said sarcastically. "Now, we need to get real, you and I. George has been very helpful on the subject of your career. He is a practicing artist, after all. Don't laugh like that."

Gabriel murmured, "He needs the practice!"

"Gabriel, you've got to learn to listen!"

"I can listen and talk at the same time."

"George lives with the difficulties. He says that the point is to combine what you're interested in with the ability to make a living for the rest of your life. You could be a show business lawyer." She was looking at him.

"Sorry?"

She went on, "These lawyers deal with creative people. Not only that—they make creative things happen. But they're never unemployed or out of fashion. They never get bad reviews. I want you to think about it. Meanwhile, I'm going to research a university where you can study law and carry on with your drama stuff, too, if you still want to do it. Then you're going to see a lawyer friend of George's. He's got money coming out of his ears. He'll explain it all to you. What's that funny face for?"

He said, "I don't want to work in an office."

"Why not?"

"Offices make me feel I'll never get out of them."

"What are you talking about?"

"You've never worked in an office."

She got up. "You've been spending too much time with your father! I want to develop your confidence. I'm afraid you're developing a kind of loser mentality!" She paid the bill and they swept out. "I must say," she said, you don't look pleased, you little bugger."

"Pleased about what?" He was following her as quickly as he could. She'd always done this, walked faster than him.

"About my new job, and the holiday in Italy and everything I've been trying to do for you. Kids—they only think of themselves. It's me, me, me, with you lot. People don't know, or won't say, how much they hate their children."

He was hardly listening. She wanted him to be a lawyer. He was, he reckoned, already sufficiently engaged with the law. In the next few days his mother would have her forged copy of Lester's picture framed and presented to Speedy, who would have been presented with two forged copies of the same picture by two members of the same family.

Gabriel's prison sentence, already long enough, would, surely, be increased. He remembered that when he visited the flats nearby, one of the men there had been in prison. "I done my bird," he kept saying. This badge of the outlaw life had been the cause of some admiration, but Gabriel couldn't remember if the man had said the prisoners were allowed to read all day. Could he take his Walkman? Would his parents visit him? How long did forgers get?

By the time they got home, his head was host to its own firestorm. He needed time to consider everything but wondered whether his mother, in one of her "concerned" moods, would want to visit a gallery, or whether she'd invite him to watch one of her favorite "uplifting" musicals with her.

Fortunately, in the late afternoon, she told him she had to go to work.

"I need to leave a bit earlier today," she said. "There's someone I think I should phone and meet with. Is that all right?" she said guiltily. "Do you mind?"

"It's fine. I want to look at my new book and draw."

"Good. By the way," she said, "I wanted to give you this." She handed him a booklet. He looked at the title—"A Career in Law"—and shivered.

"Thanks," he said. "Is that Denis Law?"

"Cut it out. Let me know what you think. It's been a lovely day, Angel. I hope we get to spend a lot of time together. If we go to Italy we will."

"He'll be there."

"Yes, George will be there."

"What for?"

"For me to be with, that's what for! You've got to stop complaining about everything." Then she said, "You're not going to be in touch with Archie this afternoon, are you?"

"Why, have you got any questions for him?"

"Gabriel—" She was holding her breath. "I presume that

was one of your jokes, which I'm sick and tired of, like the rest of this 'Archie' stuff. Now, give me a kiss. Please."

"There."

"Thank you."

When she'd gone, Gabriel did, for a while, sit in his room drawing. He drew a Japanese vase carefully but, unlike before, it failed to appear. Not that he needed a Japanese vase in his life at the moment. It was easy to wish hard and think that this made things happen. In the end, action had to be taken.

It was a relief when it didn't work. No more hallucinations; he wanted to live in the same world as other people. He wouldn't copy any more; it would be only original originals from now on. Copying had got him into enough trouble.

He put his materials away.

He found himself looking for Hannah in order to tell her that he was going out. When he saw that she had fallen asleep in front of the television, he searched the house for cash. Reluctantly he collected the money he had been saving to buy his movie camera. He raided his childhood piggy boxes, looked in the pockets of old coats, collected the money he'd earned on his paper round, and the money given to him by relatives at Christmas. He went through his mother's handbags and found a ten-pound note.

He was ready.

Leaving a note to say he had gone to Zak's, he closed the front door as quietly as he could.

Eleven

It was a thirty-minute walk to Speedy's restaurant.

Outside Splitz, behind a remorseless velvet rope and patch of red carpet, bulged an eager queue. Beyond the door, Gabriel could see people stopping to look at his "Lester" picture.

Although Gabriel had set off with good intentions, when he arrived at Splitz he began to consider it an excellent idea to go home and lie down with a pillow over his head.

He was about to turn away when a sleek car drew up outside and two men and two women got out, looking to be looked at. Gabriel watched them approach the rope; they were ushered through the crowd at the door. Gabriel knew he should know who they were, but they were gone before he could think about it.

Through the window, along with everyone else, Gabriel saw Speedy trot over to them, taking quick little steps on his high-heeled boots; he reached up to press his busy lips against their faces, before taking them to a table.

When Speedy had settled them, he returned a few minutes later and glanced in Gabriel's direction. In a moment he had stepped outside.

"You coming in, beautiful baby? I think you are!"

Before Gabriel could say anything, Speedy had taken his arm, unhooked the velvet rope and led Gabriel through the crowd. Gabriel liked that; he could get used to privilege, he reckoned.

Speedy was sitting close to him at his "operating table." At this distance, Gabriel could examine Speedy's pasty yellow glow, like the moon on an off day. Gabriel couldn't help enjoying the enthusiasm with which Speedy regarded him.

"Is there anything I can do for you, Gabriel?"

"Thanks for putting Dad onto Jake Ambler. We went over there and taught that kid a few things."

"You did? That kid's a nutter, did I tell you that? Smacked his therapist across the chops, I heard. The only music he knows about is the five-finger exercise. Ha, ha, ha!"

"It doesn't matter. It helped Dad out. He was getting pretty low about Mum and all that. Actually, he's been down to zero."

"I'm sorry to hear it. These things can get a guy down, I know. Is that what's been happening to you?"

"I suppose so."

"Yeah. How about some juice, kid? Beer? Ice cream? Not sure? What about a waitress?"

Speedy was watching him.

Gabriel said, "Right now I'll take the juice."

"OJ!" Speedy said into the air, confident that his cry would not go unheard. "Just passing by? Come in any time."

"What about the queue?"

"You don't have to worry about that. Just step right in. You're looking good. I like your hair parted like that. Funny how you're so blond and they're dark. Knew your parents well for a long time. Pretty good people." He couldn't stop talking. "Feeling lonely, eh? Sunday afternoon. I've had a lifetime of Sunday afternoons like that, with nothing on the telly but *East of Eden*. Somehow I think my whole life has been organized to avoid Sunday afternoons, followed, of course, by a Monday at school. Don't tell me how it is—I know which way up it is for a kid."

"Oh yeah?"

"You know, I was talking to a writer friend who is taking those workshop things with young people. When he asked them to write about their childhoods all the stories—every one—were about being humiliated by adults. Right?"

"Wow," said Gabriel. "It's a familiar thing, then?"

"Indeed. Look, look Gabriel—over there."

He pointed down at the table where the four people who'd come in earlier were sitting.

"There's Charlie Hero. Don't you recognize him?"

"Is that him? He's much older."

"Yeah. Your father played with him. He's with his school friend Karim Amir, the half-Indian actor, fresh out of the clinic. He's in that big film with all the sand—I can't remember what it's called. Jake Ambler produced it. There was a cool party at Gaga, and Charlie played 'Kill for Dada' with his old band. Karim got up and harmonized." Speedy put his lips to Gabriel's ear. "You know—this isn't gossip—everyone knows—"

"What?"

"Charlie's mother and Karim's father were lovers, years ago. Karim told me he caught them at it in her back garden in Beckenham, one time."

"Wow. I love those old stories. Everyone knows everyone else."

"So will you, soon. That's the way it goes. I'll see to it. She's dead now. I think the father is, too. I'm not sure. I can find out from an old copy of *Hello!* Want their autographs? Why not meet them? I'll take you over."

Gabriel looked across at Karim and Charlie, so frivolous and self-absorbed. If he had their money, he would be able to make his film; he wouldn't be sitting here.

"Maybe later," Gabriel said. "There's something on my mind." He leaned forward. Archie was right there with him, giving him strength. "I wanted to see Lester's picture."

"There it is, pal. Over there, under the light. Come in and take a good look whenever you want. We'll get you an armchair if you want to get comfortable. This is an artists' hangout."

"Lester Jones didn't give the picture to my father. He gave it to me. He wanted me to have it because he liked me. That's what people can't see, Speedy. It wasn't a money thing. It was freely given—a gift."

"What are you talking about?"

"Lester said I was talented."

"Really? At what?"

"Painting. Making films. I know how to do it—I know I do—and that's what I'm going to do. A lot of the stuff around at the moment is no good at all. I want to be the best, Mr. Speedy."

"When you grow up?"

"Yeah. On that day."

"Wow. That's an imprimatur enough for me."

"Underneath it all, Dad's talented, you see. I get it from him."

"No. If you've got it, you get it from yourself and don't you forget it. You can inherit an old tie but not a gift, that's one thing I know." Speedy was looking at him. "You think I haven't tried to write scripts and make films? I sat still at a desk for—for quite a long time; at least it seemed a long time to me—and I couldn't imagine a thing! The only thing I ever wrote was a cheque!"

"For some people, imagining is the most natural thing in the world. They don't have to sweat blood over it. You just hit the groove and see stuff!"

"You might, Gabriel. But I don't. Or, the moment I see something, I know I've seen it before in a better film than I could ever make, and there's no point writing it down again. You're one lucky guy, Mr. Gabriel." He lowered his voice. "Every idiot in this bar is trying to write a script. Not one of these people doesn't have a badly written story in their drawer. But, in the end, how many of them are really prepared to put the work in? They might be able to spell, but they can't write to save their lives. If you can really do it, you're the top man. But I know those guys, the creative artists. They're selfish and self-obsessed; the desire for success isn't pretty. It's a hunger that never goes away or can be satisfied. That's what makes people into stars."

"Mr. Speedy—" interrupted Gabriel.

Gabriel saw that Speedy, unlike most other people, didn't leave gaps in the conversation; however, he didn't seem to mind if you butted in. For him listening was an opportunity to peruse his restaurant and wave.

Gabriel continued, "I think Lester will be annoyed at the picture being here. My father shouldn't have sold it to you. It doesn't really belong to him. Dad's a good guy but he was desperate and depressed and living in a dump. He's admitted he did a bad thing. He knows he made a mistake."

Gabriel started to empty his pockets of their notes and coins onto the table.

"What do you think you're doing?"

"Take it, Mr. Speedy. Please. Let me buy it back—my picture."

"Wait. Lester was annoyed—did you say? Who gives a damn. To hell with Lester. He's got everything a guy could want. He's such a big man he doesn't even pay his taxes. Why would he worry about a picture? He could paint more pictures. That one can't have taken him more than ten minutes. Well, twenty, maybe, with the words and all."

"I'm worried about the picture."

"How can anyone worry about a damn picture?"

"That this is the right place for it."

"Wherever I am is a good place for any picture—I can assure you of that, baby. Have you got a problem, Gabriel?"

"Mr. Speedy—"

"If you want the picture so badly, there must be a reason."

Speedy was sitting close to him; Speedy was stroking his knee and going higher, into the softer flesh. Gabriel could hear Archie screaming. Gabriel told him not to be so touchy; wasn't he used to it, from school? There would be worse things.

Gabriel said, "You purchased it. You have a lot of money. But Speedy, I want to say: is there anything I can do for you?"

"Sorry?"

"Is there?"

Speedy applied the back of his hand to his forehead and made as if to swoon away.

"That, little baby, is the number one question I've been waiting for all my life! Can I have time to think about it?" Speedy was goggle-eyed and almost choking. "You are quite a kid, right! Ha, ha, ha!"

Charlie Hero passed by the table and Speedy grabbed his hand.

"Hey, Charlie, Charlie—"

"What's happening, Speedy?"

"Meet Gabriel. He's my latest pal." Charlie raised his eyebrows. "It's not what you think, Charlie. I said pal, not peach. His father's Rex Bunch, the guitar player. He was in the Push with you."

"I'd remember that, if I had a memory," said Charlie. He touched Gabriel on the shoulder. "One thing returns. We were doing open-air gigs and in the evening, when it got chilly, Rex's feet got cold. We had to put an electric heater in the wings to keep him warm. When his bunions were burning, he could play. He couldn't always stand up straight, but he could stroke those strings."

"Yeah, he's a stroker, that man. How's Karim?" said Speedy.

"He's good at the moment. Lester's laying some stoical music on his new film. And he's got a son now—Haroon, he's called, known as Harry. Then he's getting married."

"Party?"

"I should say so."

"Where?"

"Mental, I think, or Anus, maybe." Charlie lowered his voice. "Speedy—"

"Yeah?"

"Send that waitress over to ask for my autograph. Tell her not to recognize Karim or ask him for anything, right? Ask her to give me a kiss, too. These girls do kisses, don't they?"

"Sure." Charlie was laughing. "No problem." When Charlie had gone, Speedy said, "Nice guy. No talent and with the vanity of Cleopatra herself! But bright." He pointed. "His bondage trousers are in that cabinet over there. Gabriel," said Speedy, "I've heard you, man. It's gone in. It's hit the hot spot and it's workin' in me."

"What do you think?"

"If a part of me belongs to you, then a part of you has to belong to me. But which part?" Speedy was looking dangerously thoughtful. "What, precisely, do I want you to do for me?"

Then, as Speedy would have said, his eyes lit up, and stayed lit.

"Why are you staring at me?" said Gabriel.

"Full beam on!" said Speedy. "Listen up."

When he'd finished talking, Speedy stood the menu up on the table and cut Gabriel a little line of coke to help him "on his way."

Gabriel tasted it and then said, after a moment's hesitation, "No thanks. I've got a cold. Next time. But I'm grateful for everything else."

A few minutes later Gabriel was watching as one of the waiters unscrewed the picture and took it down. He wrapped it in thick brown paper, fashioned a handle from string, and handed it to Gabriel.

"There you are, sir. It's all yours. Can you carry it?"

"I think so."

Gabriel waved to Charlie and Karim but Charlie was signing a piece of paper and Karim got up and left the table.

Speedy stood there holding the door as Gabriel left.

"See you," he said. "I can't wait."

"See you," said Gabriel. "Me neither."

"Take care now. You won't go back on it?"

"No."

"Good. In a couple of weeks I'll be in touch."

Gabriel said, "I look forward to it."

"Great."

"Great."

Twelve

He was about two miles from home.

Gabriel was used to walking about the city but it was late on Sunday afternoon and the streets were packed with concentrating shoppers. In places the crowd was so tight he had to stop altogether and lean against a wall. Blasts of heat from the open doors of the bright shops and from the Underground grills in the pavement made him wonder if he weren't in hell. He believed he could easily have been carried around a shop, through the changing rooms and out into the street again without touching the polished pine floor.

The picture in its frame was cumbersome and difficult to carry. It was longer than his arm, and its edges, which had penetrated the brown paper, seemed to be made of barbed wire. Sometimes he hauled it under one arm and then under the other. For a bit he carried it on his head but it tipped backwards and if he hadn't stuck his leg out, he'd have dropped it.

His leg was inflamed; his hands were torn and sore; his arms ached. It would be awkward getting the picture through the doors of a single-decker bus, had he been able to get on one, and no cab would have stopped for him, even if he had the money. When people had bought something they simply stepped out of the shop and into the road, with an arm raised.

He turned here and there, not knowing what to do. He would never get it home. What a weight this gift had turned out to be!

He was so fatigued he became convinced his name was being called. He was thinking he'd had enough of the "hallucinations" when he saw Zak gesticulating in his face.

"Gabriel, where have you been?"

He was glad to put the picture down.

Zak was with his father and a young man with messed-up hair and drawstring combat trousers. They were laden with shopping bags. Zak's father, now wearing several studs in his ears, put his bags down and took the young man's hand. Gabriel remembered Zak saying that his father's boy lover was the same age as his daughter, Zak's older sister. If Gabriel thought his own life had become strange, he had only to contemplate Zak's in order to gain a sense of proportion.

"I haven't been anywhere," said Gabriel at last.

"It's been ages since you called me."

"I haven't had time."

It was the truth, in a way. But it made Zak annoyed.

"Too busy for us, eh?" he said. "I'm planning on making the film with Billy."

"What for? It was my idea. It's nothing to do with Billy. For a start, Billy's a bonehead."

"Right. My dad's got a little camera. I thought you'd given up."

"Why?"

Zak blushed. "You're too grand for us, hanging out with Lester Jones."

"That's got nothing to do with this," said Gabriel. "You know he's known Dad for years."

"You don't really know Lester Jones, do you?" said the young man.

"I've met him," Gabriel replied.

"I expect he's met a lot of people," he said.

"That's right," said Gabriel. "But not you." He turned to Zak, who was laughing. "I'll come round with the story-boards."

"I'll believe it when I see it," said Zak.

"Zak—" said Gabriel, grabbing him by the shoulders. "Please, believe me. I want to do it more than I've ever wanted to do anything."

"Yeah, yeah, sick of waiting for you, man."

Gabriel realized he hadn't been able to think of anything but his recent worries. What he wanted was a clearer mind, a mind that had, somehow, been on holiday.

"Look at all this swag," said Zak's father. "We've had shopping fever all day. We'll be disappointed if we don't get through at least a grand."

Gabriel had never quite worked out whether Zak's father lived with his family or not. Gabriel had the impression that sometimes he lived with one woman, occasionally with his boyfriend, and even, from time to time, with his wife. If the lives of adults were always puzzling, it was a mystery to Gabriel how such an aged and unattractive person could get anyone, except a doctor, to touch him. However, Dad had said he admired him, and Gabriel felt more open-minded, too.

"We're going home to watch the Tottenham–Sporting Depravity game," said Zak. "We've got the shirts and everything in here. Why don't you come with us?" He put his mouth to Gabriel's ear. "I'd really like you to, mate. These lovey-dovers are going to get me down, kissing all through the Depravity game and rubbing their bottoms together at the end when the players take their shirts off. I just know they'd prefer to watch a Barbra Streisland concert."

Gabriel laughed. "Maybe later. I've got stuff to do."

"Are you sure?"

"Yes. But I will come round."

"OK," said Zak. "See you, mate."

The break was useful; Gabriel continued his journey more hopefully.

It happened, after a while, that he was passing his mother's bar. He didn't want her to see him, not with the picture. But as he felt like looking at her—a glimpse of her face would ease his mind—he stood outside in an unobtrusive position.

Usually she was easy to spot, but he couldn't see her pouring long streams of alcohol into what looked like little silver thimbles. He wondered whether she was there at all. He couldn't believe she had lied to him and gone to see someone else, perhaps George. Maybe she was in the back.

A group of people moved and he saw her then, sitting at a table at the rear of the bar. She was with a man: his father.

Gabriel stared at these two ordinary people, leaning on the table, talking. His father, a wiry man who usually seemed intense, looked relaxed. At one point Gabriel's mother reached over, said something, and stroked Dad's hand. It was like an old photograph, a petrified glimpse of the past. For a moment he saw how they had liked one another long ago.

He shaded his eyes and tried to see if he could read their lips. He wanted to know if they were saying his name. Were they discussing his visions or his life as a lawyer? But he was too far away to know. Anyhow, his mind felt relieved. If they were together, worrying about each other, he could worry, once more, about his film and what he wanted to do once this was sorted out.

He picked up the picture and continued his difficult journey, inch by inch, shuffling, grunting and hurting.

Hannah said it was time to prepare his tea. She didn't ask him about the picture he had staggered through the door with, until she came into the kitchen.

He was on tiptoe on an unsteady chair on which he had placed several art books. He was attempting to push the framed picture, along with the two copies, into the back of a high cupboard.

"Ah-ha." She was standing beside the chair. She even wobbled it to emphasize her power. "You are caught like a squishy fishy on my hook!"

"Hannah—don't do that!"

"Up to something."

"Hannah—"

"Wait till your mum hears about this. You will be roast beef!"

"Don't tell her anything!" he said, wondering if, at this moment, his parents were still talking, or whether his father had returned to his room.

"I will," she said, grandly. "That's what I am given food for—to tell things about you. For more telling—more pudding!"

To balance himself he put his arms out. This was a foolish but necessary position.

"If you inform her about this, Hannah, you will be fired."

"Pah! Naughty boy! I'll tell her twice now! Your bottom will be on fire! Thwack, thwack! Ha, ha, ha!"

"Yes, but if I tell Mum that you are a rotten and cruel au pair who watches television all the time, you will be straight back in Bronchitis pulling turnips out of the frozen ground with your broken old teeth. Mum's very protective of me. Right?"

There was a silence. When Gabriel looked at Hannah from his position atop the books, he saw she was afraid. He had made his statement without thinking, and, somehow, it had worked; he had turned the key to Hannah.

"No, no," she whispered. "Please don't tell that."

"Well, we'll see."

"See?"

"How you behave. Meanwhile, I think I'll have something to eat. Help me down, please."

"Yes, yes," she moaned, holding her arms out for him to jump into. "Anything you want to eat, my boy darling?"

"A peanut butter sandwich," he said at last. "Don't forget the jam, the honey and a milkshake on the side."

"No, no," she said. "Right away coming down. Is that a vanilla or strawberry shake?"

"One of each."

"One of everything, coming up just now, no delay, number one. Is there anything else?"

He thought about it. "How about pecan pie and custard. You can have a little, too, Hannah."

"Can I?"

He nodded nobly.

"Thank you," she said. "You won't tell, will you?"

"I haven't yet decided what to do with you, Hannah. Some of your behavior can get a little weird at times. Child abuse is a very serious matter in this country. The jails are bursting with weeping au pairs but there's room for just one more!"

She moaned gently and scuttled off to fetch his food.

Hannah had just brought him a hot chocolate; he was lying in bed working on the story for his film and saying the dialogue aloud, when his mother came in that night. She had her compassionate face on, what he called her "starving children in Africa" look.

"Oh Gabriel, you're talking to yourself again! I have to tell you that I have been worried about you." She was stroking his forehead and caressing his cheeks. "What have you been doing?"

"Eh . . . working on my film."

"How's it going?"

"I'm enjoying it."

"When you actually make it, can I help you with the costumes?"

"Do you want to?"

"I think I'd love that," she said. He noticed that Hannah's considerable shadow was listening at the door. "How's Hannah?" his mother whispered.

"Why do you ask?"

"I feel guilty leaving you with her all the time. Does she respect you?"

Gabriel hesitated. Through the crack of the door he could see one of her eyes, hovering.

"I like her now," he said. "She looks after me very well."

The eye blinked several times and became watery.

"Good," said his mother. "By the way, you haven't had any contact with spiritualists, have you?"

"Sorry?"

"Archie." She said his name with care. "My dead son. The voices speaking inside you. All that. You told me about it. It . . . made me uneasy."

"Everyone has voices," he said, "but people conceal them from other people. People conceal a lot from other people. I guess it was just my 'magination."

"You don't hear from these voices all that often, do you?"

"No. Not all that often. We like to keep in touch when necessary."

"You must be lonely."

"Sometimes. What about you?"

"Am I lonely? I don't know. D'you think I am?"

"A little."

He wondered if she'd say anything about having seen Dad. It was odd how secretive parents could be, while at the same time demanding to know everything about their children.

He said, "Anything interesting happen today?"

"Same as usual," she said.

For a moment he wondered whether seeing his parents together had been a hallucination. Yet he felt sure it hadn't been. "Anyone odd come in?"

She hesitated. "Like who?"

"George."

"No."

"Does George like you?"

"He likes the idea of an older woman. He thinks there's a lot I can teach him. Maybe there is. He listens to me." She said proudly, "He tells me I'm wise."

"He flatters you. But he'd really want someone more his own age, wouldn't he? Do you think much about Dad?"

"A little. But it's best if we forget all that and think of the future."

"Dad said something to me."

"What?"

"That underneath everything . . . he loved you."

"No—"

"He did!"

She said, "He hasn't said that to me for a long time. Was he drunk?"

"Don't be stupid."

He noticed she had a strange expression on her face, of pleasure, dismay and embarrassment.

He asked, "D'you think you might see him . . . in the near future?"

"We'll see," she said. "I don't know about that man, I really don't."

He didn't ask her anything else.

Thirteen

A couple of weeks later, after school, he was surprised not to find Hannah waiting on the corner. These days she was never late. He was expecting news of an important phone call—a call that, in anticipation, made him feel both afraid and excited. He needed to know whether she'd taken it.

He had begun to walk home when he saw his father hurrying across the road, carrying his guitar and record bag, and talking into a mobile phone. Twice Gabriel had been supposed to see him recently but Dad had cancelled. "Something" had come up; he was "working."

"I rang Hannah and told her I'll walk you back," said Dad, turning the phone off. "Then I'm off to South London to teach."

"You're crossing the river?"

"It's got to be done. I'm getting all over the place and I'm enthusiastic about certain bridges and houses, funny streets, Spitalfields, Brick Lane, the City—like a tourist. When I'm out there I feel fragile, like an old man now, as if I could be easily knocked over. Yet it's as if I'm seeing it again for the first time in years. Things are turning from grey into color. I'll let you know how the weather is down south. Afterwards, I'm going to a music shop with someone who wants to buy a guitar."

Along with masseurs, drug dealers, accountants, personal trainers, language teachers, whores, manicurists, therapists, interior decorators and numerous other dependants and pseudo-servants, Dad had found a place at the table of the rich. He gave them music as others provided trousers, well-trimmed fingernails or a set of accounts. If wealth was to "drip down," as people had been told it inevitably did, it would find its level through Rex.

Dad loved the way his new work was developing, apart from the best-paid job of all, which he liked to claim he'd taken only out of curiosity. He had started to help a bunch of rich "City boys" who had a band called Boom that played at parties and friends' weddings. Dad's responsibility was to teach them to massacre great songs and instruct them in the Chuck Berry walks, Pete Townshend whirls and Keith Richards gestures they had previously confined to their bedrooms. The worst part was attending the gigs, the first of which had taken place in the country, in a tent, with the guests in evening dress and muddy patent-leather shoes. Nevertheless, Gabriel knew that however much Dad complained, he must have enjoyed the champagne, food, respect and other inevitable perks. Next time, Gabriel would go along. Dad thought he would enjoy it.

Dad was still puzzled by the fact that, although nobody wanted him to play for them, quite a few people, it was turning out, wanted to learn from him. Fortunately, what he enjoyed most of all—and he knew this straight away—was working with young people. For reasons he didn't himself understand, he could give them the attention they couldn't get from their parents. Today he was on the way to see a pupil recommended by Carlo, an anorexic ex-girlfriend of Carlo's who was learning to play bass, though she could hardly lift it, and her father who was starting the guitar.

"I've just been to the library," he said. "I'm getting out books on teaching and music. Reading's pretty interesting, you know. I wish I'd done more of it, instead of watching telly or sitting in the pub."

"What's made you start reading now?"

"To keep a few feet ahead of my students. Some of them are pretty bright. My diary is filling up. I'm taking bookings into the New Year."

Gabriel was surprised his father had a diary at all; until recently what would he have put in it? He didn't even go to the dentist. Before, when he bought a diary, he waited until March, when they were half price.

"You like teaching, don't you?" said Gabriel. "How's that little idiot who reckons he—"

"You mean Carlo? I'm starting to work him out. It's like going for a walk with a little kid. They're slow and stop all the time. They won't go at your speed. You have to go at theirs, finding their rhythm. Carlo's closed up . . . but there are chinks of light—because there are things he likes to play and to listen to. He's a fascinating case. Making him feel better—when I can see the pleasure in his eyes, makes me—"

"The pleasure in his eyes?"

"Yes. It makes me feel better, too. Whatever else goes on, learning is something healthy."

Gabriel said, "You spend more time with him than you do with me."

Dad put his arm around Gabriel. "Christ, man, is that how it feels? Have you been lonely?"

During the past fortnight Gabriel's mother had been going out most evenings when she wasn't working. She was seeing George, he guessed. One night she didn't return at all, but came home early in the morning and pretended she'd just got up.

"Sleep well?" he had said.

"Yes, thank you."

He suspected, from the anxious look on her face, and the modesty of what she wore, that she was also going out to see Dad on occasion.

When she was at home she talked on the phone for hours to her women friends. She shouted at Hannah about the state of the house, before going out again. She told Gabriel nothing about what she was doing, no doubt for "his own good."

Yet when it comes to their parents, all children are detectives, working in the dark, looking for clues and examining any evidence that might yield knowledge of these enigmas. He had heard Mum listening to her "Learning Italian" tapes. She was, too, looking at a book of Piero della Francesca paintings. He remembered George saying that Piero's "Madonna del Parto"—the young woman in the blue dress—wasn't far from his castle.

However, his "teenage mother," as he called her, didn't seem well. She looked as though she wept a lot; she was losing weight and had begun to accumulate even more self-help books; her bed was full of chocolate wrappers and she drank Tia Maria in the morning. She wasn't yet old but he was beginning to see what sort of old woman she would be, and it wasn't the picture she had presented to him in Kew Gardens. It was sadder and more desperate than that.

He was angry that she wasn't at home more. He wanted to ignore her but he needed her there to ignore; you couldn't ignore someone who didn't realize they were being ignored, or who was ignoring you. She had made up her mind that he was to be a lawyer and that was that. She thought that she had to take no other interest in what he was doing.

Dad went on, "Now I'm not living at home there's more of a distance between you and me, Gabriel. Each time we meet we have to start again. We'll have to put the effort in. But you've had a lot of me, over the years, and I have to do my job, now

I've got one." Dad pointed at the gutter. "Angel, you know where I'd be without this work."

"Is it well paid?"

"Unfortunately, yes. At the end of the lesson I'm always embarrassed when they start scribbling cheques. I want to say, 'What is this for?'"

"You don't though, do you?"

"You think I'm an idiot?"

"What have you got in your music bag?"

"It's light—and heavy. Mahler's Fifth."

"Is that all?"

"I'll only play the Adagietto to this kid—maybe a few times so he gets it in his bones," said Dad, thumping himself in the stomach.

"But you're teaching blues guitar, aren't you?"

"I've become passionate for Mahler."

"Keep that to yourself."

"The kid will understand the sadness of the piece. What d'you expect me to play him—the Supremes?"

"You love the Supremes."

"It could have been worse. I might have made him listen to that Bartók string quartet. Most of the old music bores me. The fifties not the sixties was the golden age of American music. Almost anything after that is overestimated. In my opinion, pop nowadays is panto for young people and pedophiles. But as I discovered today, the German writer Goethe said that music begins where words end. For some people words seem to make everything too clear. So I can only say—words drop dead here, pal, with Mahler!"

"Yeah?"

Gabriel was nervous that Dad's pupils would mock him as they mocked their other teachers, sneering at the maddening tangle of wires about his neck, from his Walkman, his glasses and his phone; or the way he pulled his trousers up over his belly; or at his habit of scratching his body with the backs of his fingernails, and even at his enthusiasm, as he sat there with moist eyes, collapsing and wailing over some doleful piece of Mahler at their parents' expense.

His father said, "Tell them to play it at my funeral. Something by Miles, perhaps. And that Adagietto."

Originally, the mention of his own death had been an occasion for emotional blackmail, but now Dad presented his passing away as an opportunity to consider his favorite tunes.

The bus stop was a few yards away from their house, at the top of the road. As Dad seemed agitated today, Gabriel decided to wait with him.

Dad put his hand in his pocket and gave Gabriel some money. "This is for you. I've been meaning to . . . I haven't been able to, before . . ."

Gabriel took some money and went to give the rest back. "That's all I need. I've got to pay my bill at the video shop."

"Take the lot. All I need is my bus fare. Give Mum the rest. Don't forget to say it's from me. How is the old girl?"

"Don't you know?"

"What? Maybe I do. Maybe I don't. Help me out, Gabriel—does she speak fondly of me, at all?"

"Not yet."

"Once hatred is expressed, love has a chance. Isn't that always the way? What are you doing right now? Shall we have a quick drink?"

Gabriel said, "Dad, what's up with you today? You've got that staring-eyed look. Are you nervous about teaching? What if they don't want to learn?"

"It's not difficult to see that people assume you're a sadist masquerading as an educationalist. If they don't want to learn, I sit with them—thinking."

"Thinking about what?"

"What I'm doing is teaching people how to listen to what is

going on in the music, to hear what is there. You can't make music yourself if you don't know what the possibilities are. The kids see that. The kids don't bother me. I can get straight to them, and them to me. It's the older ones and their parents I mind. Have you got a minute to talk?" said Dad. "Let's have just the one. It's not the intoxication I'm interested in—I'm parched. I only want to quench my thirst."

Dad was already hurrying across the road, towards his old local on the corner, where children were allowed until eight, and they knew Rex and Gabriel well.

The place was full of childish men from the post office and the local bus garage gazing up at the big TV screen. Dad's grey-faced mates were playing pool. They all looked the same to Gabriel, with their roll-ups, pints and musty clothes. They rarely went out into the light, unless they stood outside the pub on a sunny day, and they were as likely to eat anything green as they were to drink anything blue or wear anything pink.

Dad had hardly reached the bar before his pint was pulled and put down, next to Gabriel's St. Clement's. They sat at their usual table, where Gabriel used to do his homework while Dad talked at the bar.

Immediately Dad seemed settled: Gabriel wondered whether he really intended to give his lesson. He loved his new work, and always seemed on the point of abandoning it.

Dad drank half his pint and licked his lips. "I wanted to say—" he began.

"Game, Rex?" said one of his mates, coming over.

"Not now, Pat. With the boy."

"Gabriel," said Pat. "Rex, where you been?"

"Working."

"Working?"

Dad said, "Your surprise surprises and annoys me, Pat. Yes, working—where I'm off to when I've finished talking to Gabriel."

"Recording?"

"That sort of thing," said Dad.

"No time for your old mates?"

"I'll be back," said Dad. "Even you know that what goes up must come down. Don't you worry!"

"I am worrying," said Pat. He put his hands on the table and his face close to Dad's. He had filthy nails. "You owe me."

"Yeah, maybe I do," laughed Dad. "I expect you owe me, too. Everyone in here owes everyone else and none of them's going to get a bean!"

"You're working," said Pat. "I'm not."

"I am working this week, but I'm not carrying a lot of loose change around with me, am I, Gabriel? I can't carry the weight." Dad said, "Pat, what about when I asked if I could stay at yours and you didn't even bother to reply!"

"Not my fault, pal. The wife—"

"Oh yeah? The wife."

"At least I've still got one!"

"Thanks. I even offered to kip on the floor of your shed in a sleeping bag. I know who my friends are now."

"You're working," said the man again. "Who are you trying to kid—?"

"Look," said Dad, irritably. "Give me a break, will you? I'm with my boy. Just bugger off!"

"But you owe me!" said Pat with a horrible sense of injustice. "What's that new jacket you're wearing?"

Pat reached out and put his hand in Dad's inside pocket. Dad forced his hand away.

"Don't you feel me up!" said Dad. "You can fuck off now!"

"Give me what's mine!" said Pat.

Everyone was watching. They were used to this and were fascinated. The manager reached under the bar for his cricket bat.

"Not right now," said Dad. "You can wait a couple more

days, can't you? I always know where you are—here or in front of the telly."

"Look—" said Pat.

Gabriel was pulling out the money Dad had given him.

"Here we go," said Pat. "You've got a good, sensible boy there, man."

"No, not your pocket money," said Dad. "Put it away, Gabriel, right now!"

Pat took the money, kissed it and said, "Thank you very much." He went to the bar and ordered a drink.

"Bastard!" shouted Dad. Pat wiggled his arse. To Gabriel Dad said, "I'll make it up to you. Jesus, I'm sorry. These losers are a load of idiots. They never work but they'll take everything."

"Dad—"

"Quiet!"

"All Along the Watchtower" had come on the jukebox, even louder than the TV. At the first of Jimi's chords one of Dad's friends at the pool table looked up. Dad made a guitar gesture and ecstatically screwed up his face.

"'There must be some kind of way outta here,'" he sang. "This was all I wanted," said Dad. "To make a noise like that and have people listen to it thirty years later. It must seem pretty naïve to you. Maybe we all mythologized pop and pop stars too much, and refused to see what else is worth doing. I was thinking last night what a self-destructive period it was and how many people, gratuitously, unnecessarily, put themselves in the way of serious harm. How many of us—apart from Lester—emerged with our health and creativity?"

"You did."

"I did? I know how self-destructive I am, but as with everything else, I'm not particularly good at it." He put his hand in Gabriel's hair. "Are you making or breaking? That's all I want to know, now. It's not too late for me to say that I admire you, Gabriel."

"Me? What for?"

"You ran the school magazine. You did the debating society, and the drama society."

"Not any more."

"No, you rebelled but at least you took part. You joined in and you will again. You'll keep it together, I know you will. You'll go much further than me. I kept myself apart. I know I'm intelligent. Except that it all got lost in negative energy. I wanted to rip everything down. It was a sixties idea to piss on things, the 'straight' world, mainly. It was considered rebellious. But it meant I had a cynical soul and I wish I didn't. I haven't liked things enough. I haven't opened the windows of my soul. I haven't let enough in. If only I'd had your enthusiasm. That's all that ambition is—enthusiasm with legs. Lester must have seen that in you."

"Thanks Dad. You're—"

"No, no. I'm not." Dad leaned across the table. "Have you got any of that money left? Drink up! Let's have another one—to celebrate!"

"You'll have nothing to celebrate if you don't turn up for your class," said Gabriel.

"Forget about that," said Dad. "Pint of bitter!" he called.

Gabriel said, "What would your mum say if she could see you now? She didn't turn up to school half-pissed, did she?"

"No, well. You're right. You make me ashamed. You're good at that. But listen—before we were interrupted by that fool I was saying something important. It was Jake on the phone. In fact he gave me the phone in the first place. 'You need a phone,' Jake said. 'Here you are—you're a businessman now.' 'Am I?' I said. 'I hope it hasn't come to that!'"

"So he's looking after you?"

"Too well. Gabriel, he won't leave me alone. I've been invited to . . . to . . ."

"To what?"

"A dinner. A formal dinner party."

"Great. Free food."

"It's not great."

Dad explained that Jake Ambler was delighted with his son's progress. The boy had even spoken to him, once, without mentioning self-abuse. As a reward Jake had invited Dad to the house, along with other people he thought Dad might like: an art dealer, a movie director, a model who adored the Leather Pigs, and others.

"He mentioned the director's name. We've seen his films. He was a hero."

"That's even better, then!"

"What are you talking about? Why would he want to meet me? I'll be sitting there sweating like a dunce with nothing to say. 'What do you do?' People always ask that question at these things. What do I say? What do I do?"

"You used to say to me: the truth might be a good start."

"Gabriel, I wish you could come with me. Except that it's not a kid's thing."

"Why is it bothering you so much?"

"I'm not talented or successful or brilliant." He gestured at the pub. "I'm like these guys. Except that I feel ashamed of being ordinary. Talent's a passport—it gets you into places. Without it you go nowhere, pal."

Gabriel said, "But Jake likes you."

"I'm the only adult who can talk to that lunatic progeny of his. Because I listen to him. I'm a good ear."

"That's a gift then. How many people can do such a thing?"

Another man had been eyeing them from the bar. When Gabriel glanced over again he saw the man swinging towards them, on crutches. Dad groaned.

The man said, "I saw you pay Pat back."

"So?" said Dad. "The fucker went and stole Gabriel's pocket money. I'm really sick of this."

"What about me, Rex? I'm on Pat's floor. Can't even afford a pint."

"Jesus, what am I now, a charity? Let me get to work then I'll sort you out in a week or so, when I've been paid."

"Sort me out now," said the man.

"Later," said Gabriel quietly.

"Now!" said the man. "Look at me!"

"Is everyone in this pub a vulture?" said Dad.

"You think you're better than us! All human beings are equal even if—"

"Funny you should say that, man. I am better than you. That's one thing I do know! Better in every way! Handsome, too, and famous and—"

"Dad—"

"Whatever you do, don't end up like these people, Gabriel. They've got no hope of—"

"You're arrogant," said the man. "You're a fuckin' stuck up wanker has-been—"

Before the mood could turn even uglier, Gabriel got up, pulled his father to his feet, and got him to the door.

"But I haven't finished my drink!"

"Out, out, out!" said Gabriel, giving his father a hard shove.

"What a dump," said Rex, on the street. He was banging on the window and giving his former friends the finger through it. Gabriel was perplexed to see that Dad hadn't grown out of these "fits."

"Up your arses, mates! Losers! Kiss it, mothers!" shouted Dad. "Gabriel, don't they look like corpses ready for the grave? I won't be going in there again! The whole atmosphere is rancid, hopeless, violent! I can't believe I was ever like those men—"

"You're not. You're working."

"Yeah. Maybe. Maybe I am working. I was feeling great until I went through that door!"

"Look out!" said Gabriel. "You haven't got your glasses on but I'm telling you, he's after us!"

"What are you worrying about, boy? The fucker's got no legs!"

"No, it's Pat, with the cripple's crutch!"

"Oh yeah . . . right—" Dad shaded his eyes and leaned into the window. "I can see now! That's his yellow teeth all right!"

Gabriel ran across the road, with his father jogging and cursing behind.

At the bus stop Gabriel said, "I want you to ask Jake Ambler if he knows anyone who'll let me have a cheap 16mm camera."

"Jesus, I'm not sure about that. You know I don't like to seem more grasping than I am naturally. You'll get me fired!"

"He might be pleased to help us."

"I'll see," said Dad. "I don't even know if I'm going to get to this dinner without being carried in on a stretcher."

"You will go," said Gabriel. "And it would really help me out if you spoke to Jake. After all, if it weren't for me, you wouldn't be teaching at all."

"Thank you for pointing that out, Angel. But who will I take to the ball?"

"What am I—your pimp? Don't you meet any girls?"

"You might laugh at your old and knackered dad, but actually, one of my pupils' mothers has been taking an unprovoked interest in me. Whenever I go round there she's about to take a bath. She's rich, too. But that's premature."

The bus drew up beside them and Dad got on.

"I'll think about it," said Gabriel. "I reckon I've got a good idea!"

"Who?"

"Wait and see!"

Because he felt like it, Gabriel stood there waving until the bus had turned the corner.

Dad had gone, but to get home Gabriel had to pass the pub,

unless he went over the road, which would be humiliating. Crossing the pub window he could easily have ducked down but he didn't want to. When he went past, Pat caught his eye. Pat came to the door and Gabriel didn't flee but stood there.

"Yeah?" said Gabriel, trembling.

"You're not him," said Pat. "He's a bad, bad one. Borrowed money and won't pay it back. Make sure you don't turn out that way."

"Rather him than you, mate."

Pat was shaking his head. "Later," he said.

"Fuck you, loser!" said Gabriel. Pat raised his hand. Gabriel forced himself to laugh.

Hannah was waiting at the door.

"Welcome home, Master Gabriel."

"Thank you Hannah." He was pleased to see her.

"Your breath is out."

"Too right. Prepare the sofa please and don't forget to plump the cushions. Certain circumstances have exhausted me. I need to reconvene my energies."

"Sorry your thoughts are interrupted, but Mr. Speedy's on the phone for you."

"Now?"

"That's right."

"Thank you, Hannah. I'll take the call in private."

"I'll prepare your tea, Master Gabriel. Same as yesterday?"

"Don't forget the marmalade, Hannah."

"No, Master Gabriel. Marmalade coming up! Will you be having that with the cream?"

"Chill on the cream, Hannah—for now."

"Yes, sir."

"Hello, Mr. Speedy," said Gabriel into the telephone. "What can I do for you?"

"Good afternoon, Gabriel," said Speedy. "Sorry for the delay. How was school?"

"No worse than normal."

"Can you talk? Are you prepared?"

"Yes, sir!"

"So am I, baby. Now, listen. This is what we'll do. This is how it's going to be . . ."

Fourteen

It would take her a long time to get ready. He would help.

He knew it was an important occasion because she was playing "Ride a White Swan." In the morning Mum had taken her Ossie Clark dress—the one Clark made for her in the seventies, when she worked for him—out of her wardrobe and hung it from the curtain rail, where they both stood and admired it. The day was designed to get her into this dress, which was now a little tight at the waist. She kept patting her stomach, or "pouch" as she called it. Nevertheless, the party had started at that moment.

That night she was going to dinner at Jake Ambler's house with Dad, who had become so agitated over the whole thing he had asked his own wife—at his son's suggestion—to accompany him.

"Funny, ain't it." In the bathroom Mum was drawing her face on. Not far away, in his room, they knew Dad was also getting ready; he kept running downstairs to ring and say what he was doing. "When Rex lived here, he wanted me to stop talking. Now he's taking me to this party in order to have me talk. I wonder what's made him so keen on me suddenly!"

She was going first to a fashionable bar to meet Rex, check his look and ensure he didn't have too much to drink. They would go on to the dinner party. She didn't know what time she'd be back. She was delighted to be going out, and in a few days would start work in Splitz. It had been a long time since he'd seen her so excited.

It was a relief after the previous night, which had been the first evening Gabriel and his mother had spent together in a long time. They had gone to the cavernous, bright twenty-four-hour supermarket that had opened nearby, where you could buy movies, books and computers with your bread, have lunch or buy a whole fish. At home they cooked and ate; she let him drink sparkling wine. Then the phone rang. George was saying he wanted to come by.

"Please, later," she begged in a low voice. "When he's gone to bed."

George must have been almost outside because within a few minutes he was banging on the front door.

Gabriel had gone to sulk in his room, presuming George would stay the night and they wouldn't want him around. But Mum and George had had a tremendous row. She tried to persuade him to talk to her in the pub at the end of the street, but George, who was drunk, strung out, and in a beige suit with a taxi waiting, wanted to get away. He "chucked" Mum by repeatedly saying it was too "complicated."

"George, please tell me what you're talking about! Just give me a chance! I thought we were doing something good! You wrote to me every day!"

"I'm not ready, and I will never be, for the trials of bourgeois respectability."

"You mean the boy, don't you?"

"You never talk about anything else!" he cried, almost dashing out of the door.

"You're jealous!"

"Maybe. You're a tight little family! Let's keep in touch!"

She ran out into the street after him, pleading. From the window Gabriel watched George shake her off, like someone shooing away a dog trying to bite them.

For a moment she lay down on the path, her face resting on the pavement. She looked up to see Gabriel watching her, got to her feet, shook her head and went to him. He cuddled her.

They put their pajamas on, got into her bed, watched *Frasier* and ate chocolates from their "emergency" supply.

"You didn't *like* him, did you?"

"A little bit, yes," she said.

"Well, if it was too complicated . . ."

"You were the complication."

"I was the excuse."

"Shut up now, Frasier and Niles are going to—"

Gabriel was licking his chocolate. He said, "Would you have gone with him if he had wanted you to?"

She thought for a long time. "Probably, Gabriel."

"Even if I wouldn't have liked it?"

She was stroking his hair, which he hated, and said, "It's not your job to make my life impossible. I've looked after you and now you're nearly grown. That was my duty, and I've done it. Surely, now, I can live for myself a little bit, eh?"

"OK, OK," he said. "Sorry it didn't work out."

She said, "I think, in the end, that love is probably a young person's addiction. I can get by without it—I'll have to, won't I?—but probably not without some companionship."

Now she sat at her dressing table, pulling her tights on.

He asked, "What shoes are you going to wear?"

"Look."

She went to a carrier bag and pulled from it a pair of white patent leather boots.

"Where did you get those?"

"They're real seventies boots. A woman at work collects antique clothing and she lent them to me. Do you like them?"

"They suit you."

"You think so?"

"Oh, yes."

"Just pull on those zips for me, dear."

Wiping his quivering hands on his jeans, he did as she asked. He saw himself in her mirror, watching her adjust the boots.

"I know what your dad will say: 'Puss in Boots.'" They were laughing. She kissed Gabriel. "I'll tell you all about it in the morning. What will you do?"

"Oh, I guess I'll be staying in with Hannah." He went to the window, looked up and down the street several times, and yawned. "I'll watch the rest of that Polanski and get my head down."

"Sleep well, Angel."

"Have a good time without me."

When she'd gone he had gathered his drawing materials together and was getting changed when Hannah knocked on his bedroom door.

"Come."

"It must be a mistake, Master Gabriel."

"What sort of mistake?"

"At the door there's a chauffeur waiting, with a fat car outside."

"It's impertinent to think that that would be a mistake."

"Sorry. What is this impert?"

"Look it up later."

He picked up his bag. He had packed a small hunting knife as well. But he had been to school; at least he knew how to handle himself. Not that he was worried, anyway.

"Gabriel, is it really for you?"

"I have an important meeting. Not one word to anyone, or else . . ."

"No, no, Master Gabriel. No turnip on horizon. Your shoes . . . should I clean them spotless?"

"No thanks, they're new trainers. Could you get them out of the box and thread the laces?" Gabriel said, "I've got to do this thing, Hannah, tonight. I promised I'd do it. But I'm scared, really scared. Nothing like this has happened to me before."

"Go," she said. "Go and do it."

"Yes. You're right."

"But don't be back late."

"No. See you later."

The chauffeur held open the car door and took Gabriel's bag. As Gabriel slid into the soft white leather seats, he saw Hannah at the door with her mouth open.

"Driver," said Gabriel casually. "Can you adjust the music— upwards, please!"

They zipped around the Westway, over the top of Ladbroke Grove and the Portobello Road, and through the City. Gabriel was driven to an area of narrow streets and old warehouses, where Speedy lived in a conversion. The brickwork had been scraped, the piping painted blue.

He went up in an industrial lift.

At the top, dragging open the latticed gate, Speedy greeted him.

"Welcome, Maestro!"

"Thanks, Speedy!"

"Take a look at everything! The view! The river! The pink settee! I'm exhausted—I've been clearing up for hours. My housekeeper's gone to have a sex change."

"Oh, dear."

Gabriel pushed through a plastic-beaded curtain to find himself standing on a shining patch of Astro-turf. Ahead of him was a fluffy white rug with other challenges to come.

Gabriel walked about. Speedy collected objects that Gabriel thought anyone sensible would hate—china dogs and plastic Mrs. Thatcher dolls, for instance, and anything involving winking lights. Gabriel couldn't make out whether the stuff was from gift shops or art galleries. Gabriel liked being confounded; he even liked hating things, but this—

"It's certainly made you wonder," said Speedy.

Gabriel noticed the piles of books on photography, painting, architecture and design. It was like seeing a huge chocolate cake; he wanted it all inside him as soon as possible.

"I could hang out here," he said.

"You're welcome to."

"I like the music. What is it? Sounds like trains."

"Steve Reich."

"Who?"

"Take it with you," said Speedy. "Your dad'll know about it."

"R 'n' b's his thing. But thanks. I think we'd better start."

"Gabriel, what d'you want me to wear?"

"Your favorite clothes. How you like to be seen."

Speedy put his hand on Gabriel's arm. "Oh, I don't know. I can never choose. Come and help me."

"I can't stay long," said Gabriel.

"Right, butch," pouted Speedy.

While Gabriel prepared, Speedy went to get changed. Standing there, Gabriel was startled by a smooth-skinned Thai boy or girl in a sarong and makeup, who saw Gabriel, rushed into the bathroom, and never emerged.

When they'd agreed on his clothes and the color of his lipstick, Speedy took up a position on the chaise longue, supported by Elvis-print cushions. Gabriel was a little surprised at Speedy's pose—lying on the couch with one hand behind his neck, as though he were sunbathing.

If that was how he saw himself, it was how Gabriel would paint him; if Speedy didn't like the result, that was up to him.

An angry ball of fluff ran across the floor.

"You got rats here, Speedy?"

"Don't you dare!" said Speedy. "I want my beautiful Xavier in it. In the olden days people were always painted with their houses and horses and stuff."

"I can't do dogs. That one's not going to sit still and it'll come out looking like a hedgehog. Speedy—you look powerful on your own."

"Is that right? OK, I'm going to trust you on this—"

"That's the way."

"But I'm telling you, Angel, this one isn't for the attic! It's for the front of the restaurant. I want it to look like me, only better. You know the kind of thing. I don't want my blemishes immortalized."

"What blemishes?"

"What a sweetheart you are! Who's your favorite painter right now?"

"Lucian Freud."

"But he's very . . . realistic. And I'm a vegetarian." Speedy started to laugh. "You're joking, I know you are. You're quite a kidder, kid. You won't leave my ring out, will you?"

"Where is it?"

"You'll see, baby. Coming up. Open your eyes."

"Wow."

"Yeah, told you."

"Must have hurt."

"That was the idea. D'you want one?"

"I'm thinking of a tattoo, that's all. A panther or something."

"Whereabouts?"

"Let's not get into that, Speedy."

"Right you are. I'll zip this up then."

"You do that."

Sitting on an animal-print covered chair, Gabriel wanted to work quickly, making preparatory studies for the picture. He had a few hours, for his mother would be out late. He had to be home before she returned, in case the alcohol made her sentimental and she had no one else to take in her arms at two in the morning.

"Can I talk?" said Speedy. "I'm so excited."

"You're always excited."

"Not like this. What do you want—gossip or autobiography?" Gabriel smiled. Speedy said, "Everything, then. If you're going to paint me, you're going to have to get to know me. Well, dear, when I was at your peachy age I became Jimmy McEnroe's lover. He was in his late thirties then, and one of the top pop managers of the time. He wanted me to assist him, and assist him I did, baby. I got to know all the stars. Oh Gabriel, I always wanted to be a star. I never made it to that one."

"Speedy you are a star, in the restaurant."

"I'm the boss. That's different. People want something, or they know me from last time. Gabriel, Jimmy was outrageous, until he went the way of a lot of our people, as I am going to. Still, I had a time and a half. All pop comes straight up from the gay underground. I know you're not that way, Gabriel, and it's a shame and a waste but I won't hustle you, baby. In another way you're one of us."

"Thanks."

"When I left Jimmy I . . ."

Speedy didn't stop talking. He seemed to like being looked at, though Gabriel wished he wouldn't keep craning his neck to try to see what Gabriel was doing.

"You've got to keep still."

"I'm aching," complained Speedy. "I've never sat still before. I should be painting you!"

If this annoyed Gabriel, he was already so disgusted by every line he drew he wanted to either rip up his drawings and stamp on them or run from the building. He knew he'd never get to what he wanted to do. This wasn't Speedy's fault: his mixture of naïveté and cunning, of knowingness and vanity, made him a beautiful subject. But Gabriel was beginning to learn that any attempt at art would be held up by inhibitions, terror and self-loathing. He was pushing against a closed door, and the door was himself.

At the end, he was pleased to see there must have been a score of screwed-up balls of paper on the floor. He'd done enough for today; he couldn't go any further. He knew how to go on.

When Gabriel said he was ready to go, Speedy said the car was waiting but that he needed a lift himself. Gabriel sat and listened to music while Speedy got changed again.

They drove to what Gabriel recognized as Jake Ambler's house. The lights were on; figures moved about in the big glowing rooms.

"Coming in?" said Speedy in the stationary car. "You'll know the people. What's wrong? Are you afraid?"

"I should be, but I'm not. Tonight I could do anything. You think I wouldn't want to walk through that door and talk and hang out for hours? But my parents are in there, and they think I'm at home in bed."

"Who with?"

"I wish."

Speedy said, "Is it true? Are your mum and dad together? I thought they'd—"

"Not a word to them about our work."

"My lips are zipped, my wings are clipped, my arse is whipped. Give me a kiss—I've shaved."

"Just a little one, Speedy, to thank you."

"Yum, yum . . . be my vanilla pillow, baby." Speedy was looking at him. "Come over for supper when you've finished the picture. I know some people who'd like to meet you. People who are more cultured than me—just a silly ol' queen who serves hamburgers and has never read a book in his life. They'll introduce you to all kinds of stuff and you can have conversations that'll open your head up."

"Thanks Speedy, I would like that. I will come. Look—"

A car drew up in front of them. The door was opened and crouching Lester got out, fit and purposeful, followed by Karim Amir in a black suit. Lester went to the house, where Jake greeted him. Gabriel saw Carlo in the hallway, watching Lester move towards him.

Karim came to Speedy's car and put his head through the window.

"Hi, Creamy," said Speedy. "Your hair's getting long again. Suits you."

"You sure?"

"Oh yes. Lovely texture, too. This is Gabriel. He's a film-maker. His dad played with Lester and then with Charlie."

"Lucky him. How you doing, Gabriel?" He and Karim shook hands. "Coming in, Speedy?" Karim said.

"On my way." Speedy hurriedly gathered himself together. "Oh God, look—now there's Marianne Faithfull! I'm so excited. I'm in here for a bit with the superstars. Then I'm off to the sauna. You can stay there all night."

"I'd like to see those places."

"You would? You should see everything. I'd look after you. We'll talk, baby."

Gabriel said, "Speedy, Lester might not remember me, but if he does will you thank him for the picture and for the things he said?"

"Certainly."

Speedy went off with Karim, tripping and panting.

Gabriel got out of the car and leaned against the railings outside the house, staring into the furnace of the chandeliers, but could make out little.

"You see?" he was telling Archie. "That wasn't too bad, eh? Didn't we have a good night?"

He wondered again how his life would have been different had Archie lived, and how the two of them would have influenced and loved and hated one another. He missed him.

Gabriel looked up to see a servant coming to close the shutters.

It wasn't as late as Gabriel had thought, and he asked the driver to take him for a spin around London. Gabriel imagined the car's silver grille grinning like sharks' teeth as they ate up the city. When he was older, he would do this all the time, with his friends beside him.

As they drifted past the landmarks, Gabriel fell into a dream of the future, imagining his adventures, the films he'd make and scripts he'd write. He thought of the actors, musicians and producers he'd work with, the interviews he might give and what he'd say on television; he thought of where he would live, the parties he'd attend, the dissipations he'd be prone to and the women he would meet; he wondered whether he'd work in America or not and about the mistakes it might be profitable to make, and those to avoid. Like Lester, he would do fascinating things all the time!

What a bright place London was, he thought. Here anything could be achieved! You only had to wish high enough!

Of course, he wondered if he might fail at what he wanted, as his father ultimately had. A lot of people wanted to be someone, but who had the tenacity, the commitment, the steely determination? For how many people was it a necessity, a matter of life as opposed to death? He was too young to be careful. He was full of hope and the ambition of uncontainable wishes. He was ready, too, to work. Recently he'd had ideas for two or three projects that he hadn't had time to consider properly. He wanted to write and draw new things. He saw now how bored he'd been recently, at home; he'd just about had enough of being alone and worrying about his parents.

At home he listened to the CDs that Speedy had given him.

He went happily to bed but seemed to have only just shut his eyes when he had a nightmare.

He was sitting with his mother and Archie in a bus beside his father's coffin. Other customers sat on the bus as usual. The bus conductor asked Gabriel's mother for their fares but she had no money to pay. The family couldn't take Dad's body to the cemetery in a hearse because they couldn't afford that either. Then his father, as a ghost, was sitting with them, holding Archie's hand and telling them all not to worry. Mum's friend George, surrounded by a swirling halo, was waving through the window.

Gabriel cried out but it made no difference; no one could hear.

Gabriel touched something soft. It was a real person. Gabriel was so disorientated that he reached for the light switch. But someone else's hand had made it first.

It was Dad in evening dress with his bow tie as floppy as an old daffodil. He was crumpled and smelled of alcohol and cigars. Around his mouth was something like chocolate cake.

"We've just come in from the party. You're safe. Everyone's safe. Angel, you can go back to sleep."

"You are here. It's really you. But why are you here?"

"You'll be the first to hear about it, tomorrow."

Fifteen

His father was at the table, in his usual place, with mustard and butter, and Branston pickle and ketchup and salt to hand. Underneath was the newspaper, open on the sports page; Dad moved the objects around in order to read the part of the page he required. He was listening to Verdi's Requiem while wondering aloud whether Nottingham Forest would make it to the Premiership.

Occasionally he looked up in puzzlement; he'd never been in the house with Hannah there. Unintentionally, she kept making him laugh. Gabriel could see how nervous she was by the fact that she kept raising food to her mouth, and putting it down again, as if she couldn't believe that the world had tilted once more.

Dad said, "It's funny you dreaming about me, Gabriel. I thought I saw Archie last night."

"What?"

"I was sitting there with friends when I became convinced your twin was looking through the window of Jake's house. I even made an excuse, went outside and walked about. There was no one there, of course. Weird, eh? By the way, what's this about you and Archie talking and stuff?"

Gabriel hesitated but said, "He's with me, Dad."

"Of course he is. He's with me too. That's where the kid should be, with his family."

"You talk to him?"

"Every day." Gabriel was relieved. Dad went on, "Don't tell Mum. It upsets her."

When Gabriel's mother joined them, Hannah went and stood across the room, folding clothes with ostentatious care.

"I can't wait to hear how it went last night," said Gabriel. "Did you get champagne at the door?"

"Champagne and canapés, of course."

"Then what did you eat?"

"Wait a minute. I have to give you good news," said his mother. She was in her dressing gown and her hair was everywhere. She must have been tired after last night but she seemed content. "Your father was too sensitive to ask about the camera. But I did. It turned out that years ago Carlo's father, Jake, was a camera assistant, and he's got what you want in his garage. He'll show you how to use it."

"I'll be able to start my film?"

"He suggested you shoot it over the summer. The days will be longer. There'll be more light."

Dad said, "Fluffy, you forgot." She blushed at the name. It had been a long time since he'd called her that. "Someone else was there last night, too." He was looking at Gabriel. "A friend of yours."

"That's right," said Mum. "Lester Jones turned up, for drinks. He asked how you were getting on."

"He did?" Gabriel said, "He didn't mention anything else?"

"He's doing a concert in a small venue in London and has invited us to visit him backstage."

"That's great," said Gabriel. "I'm pleased. He didn't mention the picture?"

"No." Mum was regarding Dad with annoyance. "Oh, God," she said. "I'd forgotten what a noise you make when you eat. You sit back—you're thinking, I suppose—and there's a sort of animal chewing."

"I'd forgotten what a noise you make when you're talking," said Dad. "And I'd forgotten the pleasures of living together. Was it like this all the time?" Mum lowered her head. "By the way, Christine, I wanted to ask you—who's George?"

"What?" said Mum.

Gabriel and his father were watching her.

Dad said, "Last night Gabriel was shouting in his sleep about George. Who is he?"

Gabriel was aware that Dad knew who he was. Dad was getting himself worked up.

"No one," said Mum. "There's no George."

"There better not be. Is it true, Gabriel? And don't lie to me."

Mum said, "Don't forget, Jake invited us to his country place. He's had the new indoor pool installed and thinks we might like to try it out."

"All three of us?" said Gabriel. "Are we going?"

"Would you like to?"

"Yes. I can work there."

Dad got up. "We'll see," he said. "Anyway, I haven't got time to gossip."

While Gabriel sat next to his mother and asked her to describe the previous evening's food, as well as the plates, clothes and conversation, Dad picked up his bag and went to the door.

"I've got a lot of work to do today," he said. At the foot of the stairs he turned. "I'd like to get started while I'm here, if that's all right, Christine."

Mum was looking at him. She wasn't sure.

"All right," she said at last. "There can't be too much harm in it." When Dad had gone upstairs to the bedroom she said, "I did invite him here, but he seems to be getting comfortable again."

"What's wrong with that?"

She got up and walked about restlessly. "I loved him for a long time. I loved him far more than he loved me. But it was hopeless. He was kind of gone. So I turned it off. Now he's decided he wants to start again. I was about to begin a new life."

"Maybe you will, now, together."

"You're soppy, Gabriel. What makes you think I'm such a pushover?"

"Give him a chance. He's trying to do something now."

"Why the hell should I?" She relaxed a little. "Just tell me—whisper—what 'work' is he doing in there? After breakfast in the old days, when you'd gone to school, he'd read the paper on the couch, and ask what was for lunch. How do I know he's not doing that?"

"He'll be playing music and making notes about his pupil's progress. He keeps a file on each one. I've seen them."

"He's taking it very seriously."

Gabriel said, "He's decided that making music and talking about it—the whole thing—is therapeutic."

"How can it be? I've known musicians who've been playing since they were teenagers and they're still a bunch of dead-heads." She sighed. "Still, have you noticed how much Rex's limp has improved? He's become a fortunate man, your father. He's found something at last that he's good at. I'm jealous."

"How can you be? Of what?"

"I suppose I believed that only talented people had a voca-tion or were important, while the rest of us were slaves. Your dad isn't exceptionally talented and often he's paralyzed within. But it doesn't mean he can't be useful."

"He is very useful," said Gabriel. "He's gone off the dole.

He's even given me money. Maybe he'll give you some, if you beg nicely."

"D'you think so? How much does he get paid?"

"I'm not sure—"

"Aren't you? Per hour, right?"

"I think it's—" Gabriel told her the figure.

"Is that it? That's not much more than I earn," she said.

"Jake pays more. He just gives Dad what he feels like giving him. I don't think Dad knows how much to expect. He feels ashamed, asking every time."

"He shouldn't have to put his hand out. He must send a bill. I'll do it on the new computer we're getting. I bet he's not paying any tax. He'll get into trouble. I'll sort it out. Now I'd better go and see my girlfriends. It's our coffee morning. They'll want to hear about last night."

There was a café nearby where she and her friends had met for years. They'd talk about husbands, kids, movies and TV; they'd compare what they'd bought in the antique market, and they'd give one another advice.

Before she went out she said, "Last night Rex was really sweet and polite. He held my hand—he knows I love that. He even talked to me and took an interest in what I have to say, probably because he was too scared to talk to anyone else. He promised to buy me some new clothes. If only it could always have been that way."

Later that morning, when Dad emerged from the bedroom and left to give Carlo his lesson, Gabriel accompanied him to see Jake's camera.

Dad had a hangover. On the way they stopped for coffee. The café was on the main road and it wasn't warm, but they sat on iron chairs outside, drinking juice and watching people. Dad liked to count the lunatics.

"There's one," he'd say, nudging Gabriel. "And look at that nutter, chattering and gurgling! He's got no chance, poor guy."

It seemed to reassure him to realize he was less messed up than other people.

Then Dad said, "It was really good last night, Gabriel. You might have guessed, your mother and I have been meeting a bit, just to see what's there. To see if we get on."

"And?"

"Yeah, we do get along, at times. Anyway, last night, after she invited me to come home with her, I was getting undressed. I found her dressing gown behind the door, where it always was. I showered and cleaned my teeth and all that. I started to think: she's in bed, she's waiting for me. She'll be hot in there, practically boiling—she's a high-temperature woman, at night—and soon I'll be snuggling up to her back, her legs, her arse, which is like a two-bar electric fire. Her feet will be on my legs, touching me, and that's where I want to be, kissing her neck. Excuse the details, but I'm telling you, Angel, that's what a man wants at the end of the day—and at my time of life—when he lays his tired head down. To know that a woman has chosen you, that she wants to be with you—it's an achievement."

"You don't live together."

"We'll see about that." He went on, "People are rarely a perfect fit. These days they walk away from one another too quickly. Why does everyone have to break up? If you can sit still through the bad bits you can find new things. For me, being with her again is like having a new girlfriend. Your mother suffered a lot over Archie. She deserves a break. I don't like her being a waitress. What I want is to support her financially, so she can do what she wants. I'd be proud of that." He looked at Gabriel. "You're not listening. You're thinking about something else altogether."

"Yes. I can concentrate on the things I really want to do."

"But I still don't know whether she'll have me back. I'll have to keep thinking of what might seduce her."

At Jake's, Dad and Carlo went upstairs to work.

Gabriel was standing in the hallway when Jake himself, accompanied by a uniformed servant, and wearing a suit and shoes so elegant they were, in effect, golden slippers, led Gabriel into the low garage at the side of the house. There sat two green Lotuses, a Jag and a Bentley.

Behind the cars, Jake found the big camera. He removed his jacket, put a sheet down, opened his tools, and took the camera apart on the floor. He wanted to "reacquaint" himself with it. As he rebuilt it, he talked of the films it had been used on and the famous actors it had photographed. Then Jake asked Gabriel about the film he intended to make. Gabriel recounted the story, becoming excited as he talked. He hadn't forgotten it; in fact the little movie had become clearer in his mind.

"Sounds like a pretty good contemporary movie to me," said Jake, nodding. "Full of funny detail, too."

Afterwards, in Jake's office, surrounded by movie posters, awards and an Oscar—"Everyone should have at least one of these," he said, patting it—Jake showed Gabriel stills from the films.

"Why don't you take these with you?" he said, wrapping them in tissue paper. "They're more use to you than they are to me."

"Jake, why didn't you become a director?" Gabriel asked, putting them in his bag.

"Good question," began Jake. "I think it's because I knew Jimi Hendrix, when he lived in Notting Hill."

Gabriel almost choked. "What?"

This was how Jake liked to talk, impressing the kid. For Gabriel it was like someone saying they'd been on holiday with Shakespeare.

Jake said, "I'm that old, I saw Jimi play a lot of times, at the Marquee and those places. I thought, I'll never be a genius like this guy. Who do we have to turn to these days for spiritual guidance? Not the priests, politicians or scientists. There are only artists left to believe in. So: I am a supergroupie. I love those artists who pant after chimeras. But I'd rather puff a cigar in an easy chair myself. It's my loss—doing art gives a man big balls. It's probably never occurred to you that you can't do things. But I never had the confidence to believe I could be talented, or had an imagination."

"Where did it go?"

"I had it once, you think? As a child, perhaps. I don't know. I was sent away to school. Must have been refined out of me."

"Jake—"

"Something on your mind? You're looking tense today."

"Yeah . . . Mum's got this strange idea."

"What's that? Tell me, Gabriel."

"She's started thinking that I should be a lawyer. A show-business lawyer, you know. Doing contracts for bass players and stuff."

"Yeah." Jake seemed to understand immediately. In fact he found it funny. "That's what I was supposed to be."

"And you'd recommend it?"

Jake stuck his tongue out. "What's the point of doing something you hate?"

Gabriel said, "I want my work and my life to be the same thing."

"That's what the successful people—like Lester Jones— have. Most people don't find out until it's too late what they want to do."

"Or who they want to be?"

"That's right. Why don't I talk to your mum? I'll take her out and explain what your prospects might be if you work hard and do well."

"Have you got time?"

"I can't think of anything that's more important than the future of young people like you."

When Carlo and Dad had finished and came downstairs,

looking relaxed, Jake said that when Gabriel was old enough he would get him a job on a movie as a "runner."

To Gabriel's surprise, Jake did keep his word about Mum.

A few days later Gabriel returned from school to find her at home. Her face was flushed; she'd been drinking but she was cheerful. Dad was in the kitchen, making tea.

"I've just got in," she said. "Guess what happened! Jake called this morning and asked me out to lunch. I've been on more dates in the past few weeks than I have for years. Where are you going to take me?" she called to Dad.

"You wait and see," he said. "Is it all right, Gabriel, if I go out with Mum for a bit?"

"Sure. Mum, what did Jake say?"

"He rang me up out of the blue and said he wanted to take me to the Ivy. I couldn't refuse! I called up work and said I wasn't well. What a place the Ivy is! I was looking around at everyone so much I hardly heard a word he said. Danny La Rue was there, looking great!"

Gabriel said, "What did Jake want?"

"He was praising both my boys. Said Rex was a great teacher for waking up his lad and everything. And you— well . . . He seemed to think you wouldn't necessarily make a lawyer. It would be a waste."

"What did you say?"

"All that matters to me is that Gabriel doesn't turn out like his father."

Dad didn't find this amusing.

Mum was blushing. She said, "Jake promised to keep an eye on you, Gabriel. Like a godparent. What an impressive man that Jake is. His head—in fact his whole damn body—should be on a stamp."

"Then you could lick it," said Dad.

"Gabriel," said Mum. She was laughing. "We'll leave you alone for a bit, OK? See you later."

When his parents had kissed him and left, Gabriel told Hannah he was going out. She hardly listened. She was sitting in a chair singing or moaning to herself.

Gabriel went to Splitz to sketch and photograph Speedy in situ. Gabriel wanted to finish the portrait; he had been thinking that Speedy would appreciate his restaurant being in the picture. The chaise longue wasn't quite right. He'd take Speedy's head and put it somewhere else. Wasn't that called having an imagination?

After a couple of hours' sketching and observation, Gabriel told Speedy that the preparatory work was complete. He didn't need to see him again in the—here he could only hesitate—flesh. He would, in a few weeks, give him the finished painting.

Sitting at his "operating table," Speedy was disappointed. "But I love posing for you, Angel. One more time, surely?"

"Sorry, Speedy, your face is etched in my memory."

Speedy clapped his hands and said he couldn't wait to see the picture.

Gabriel warned him, "You don't know, I'm still only a kid and it might be terrible."

"The more terrible the better! Ha, ha, ha!" Then Speedy said, "Have you told your parents what we're doing?"

"No. No I haven't."

"Thought not. I guess your mum will be all right about it. But your father probably won't like the picture and he won't like you spending time with me. He'll imagine all kinds of stuff."

"I'll tell him when I'm ready, then."

"That's right." Speedy was watching him. "What are you thinking?"

"What?" Gabriel said, "I was thinking that if I were taking photographs at the moment I'd only photograph people in close-up. I'd be so close I'd only get part of their ear, the tip of their nose or a patch of skin. I wouldn't be able to get all of them in. Why's that?" he asked, confident that Speedy would know the answer.

"You're too close to your parents. You can't see them—they're on top of you."

"Yes . . ."

"When it comes to other people, it's always difficult to get the distance right."

"Yes."

"Now you've got something to think about. D'you want a taxi?"

"Yes, I'd better get home."

When he went into the house, Gabriel heard an unearthly noise. Thinking someone was being slaughtered, he ran into the kitchen. Hannah was weeping.

"Hannah! Has someone died? Tell me what's wrong!"

She didn't want to talk. He made her a cup of tea, gave her some cake and eventually she gave way.

"It's worse than dead! Your mama and dadda are again together as one! Your father is carrying his things here."

It was true. Every few days Dad would "accidentally" leave something in the house, "until next time." The place was beginning to resemble its former condition.

Gabriel explained, "It's only a trial period."

"Wha?"

"To see how it goes."

"Suppose it goes too good?"

Mum had explained to Gabriel that she couldn't help having reservations about Dad. It wasn't that she doubted he had "progressed in his growth," it was whether any couple could eliminate the years of habit that had accumulated between them. She was, after all—and she hated to admit this—used to regarding Dad as a "bit of a fool." There was the habit of disliking him; the habit of calling him lazy; the habit of trying to push him to do things; the habit of considering him a failure. He, too, had his own way of seeing her, as a petty nag, for instance, with a conventional mind.

There was a lot for his parents to get over; it would be big work for both of them.

Gabriel liked to think he was nudging things along by informing Mum that the mother of one of Dad's pupils was so interested in him she had decided to take up music. When Dad asked, "What instrument are you thinking of learning?" she replied, "Oh, anything that involves four hands." She had even begun to give Dad gifts.

"What sort of gifts?" Mum asked.

"Oh, just little things," Gabriel said, helpfully.

"Little things, eh?" She hummed to herself but said no more. He knew she had taken it in when she bought Dad a new bag in which to carry his files, music and books.

Now Hannah went on, "I know they won't want me here any more."

"There's always someone left out, I suppose."

"It's me!"

"Why don't you want to go home?"

"I don't! I don't! First Communists—now gangsters!"

He fetched her a drink and said, "I'll talk to Mum about it, if you want. She might be able to help fix you up with something else—people even better than us."

"Would you? Oh Master Gabriel, I'd be so grateful!"

This time she kissed him.

His parents were back late. As Gabriel worked, he could hear them murmuring in the kitchen below. He was intending to go down and talk to them, but their voices grew more raucous, with sudden hushes followed by mysterious lulls. Soon, the teacups in the cupboards started to rattle. The windows would be next; a love-storm was approaching.

Sixteen

Gabriel was deputed to accompany his father to his old room. Dad hadn't been there for a few days. He'd been staying "at home."

After they'd climbed the stairs and pushed the door, Dad stood there sniffing and looking contemptuously at the familiar detritus. He took a few steps.

"I don't even want to touch my own things. I'd just as soon leave them. Everything seems coated in grease. Mum wants me to keep this place in case things don't work out between us. But I think they will. She seems to be into it, don't you think?"

"Yeah, I think so."

Mum had, Gabriel knew, been out with George. He could tell that George had rung because of the speed with which she'd dressed and got out of the door. The night this happened Dad had rung from the other side of London, where he was working. Gabriel had said she was at work, but Dad had already tried there. Dad kept ringing, until Gabriel went to bed and put the answering machine on. She came home late but alone, and, when he crept to her door and looked through, she was staring at the ceiling miserably. That was the end, he guessed. He knew for certain it was over when she abandoned Italian and started to wonder whether it was too late for her to become a primary school teacher.

Now Dad said, "Even if things don't work out and she asks me to leave again, I'll never live in this room again. I'd sleep on the street or stay with a student, if it came to it. There were times in here," he sighed, "when I felt everything had been taken away and I had nothing to live for. That time after we'd been to Speedy's, and I'd sold him the picture . . . It was an all-time low, in my opinion. I hope nothing like this ever happens to you, Angel. It certainly reduces a man."

"Yeah. Dad, let's get started."

"Right."

The first thing Dad did was remove the picture of the chair Gabriel had given him. Dad folded it up neatly and put it in his inside pocket.

"Now," he said in a conspiratorial voice. "This is how we're going to get the stuff out."

"Sorry?"

Dad explained that as he wasn't quite up to date with the rent, and didn't intend to be, they had to make an "alternative exit."

They gathered everything up, took it downstairs and, while Gabriel acted as lookout, carried it out through the back door of the house in rubbish bags. They regained the street by a side entrance. The van, driven by the old pal of Dad's who'd taken his possessions in the other direction, arrived just as someone came out and saw them.

They collected Dad's other things from his friend's garage. By the afternoon, his father's clothes, guitars and other instruments, Grateful Dead posters and books were back home. Hannah was asked to help; she shed a tear as each object was returned to its old place. The house seemed crowded and Dad's cheerfulness was tiring.

"I'm glad to be back here and in charge of everything again," he declared, slapping Mum on the arse.

"I've never liked being whacked like an old donkey."

"Come on, Fluffy," he said. "You're not an old donkey, you're my wife."

"Wife? We're not married."

"I don't think I'm ready."

"That's right. Like most men you're too immature."

"It's only that you don't have a sense of humor."

"That's because you never say anything amusing."

"Christine, other people laugh at my jokes."

"Give me their names and addresses. They're just being polite, Rex."

"Why would they be?"

"To get away from you as soon as possible. Or they're your students, fawning over you—"

"That's respect. Now, listen—"

She said, "I think I'm getting a migraine—"

As Gabriel went to the door and out into the street, he could hear their voices growing quieter and quieter behind him. This story of his parents was one he thought he might turn into a film, in the future. If only he didn't have to live through it first.

He went to call on Zak, who said, "Hey, where have you been all this time? Come in, come in!"

Gabriel almost fell through the door. "It's good to be here. Fuck, I should have come before."

"Where have you been?"

"Oh, God, I've had enormous parent stuff going on," sighed Gabriel.

Zak knew from experience what galling work this could be.

Every time his parents went out, Zak feared they'd come back with more of what he called "steps." He had stepsisters, stepbrothers and stepuncles all over London, as well as half, quarter and one-eighth brothers and sisters, the mementoes of repudiated parental passion. Sometimes he wondered who in their circle he wasn't related to. His mother, for instance, had just had a baby with a friend of her husband's, a man she no longer saw.

"Explains everything," Zak said. "Wounded, eh? Me too."

They picked their way through the house. The expensive furniture was at odd angles, and there was a goldfish bowl in the middle of the floor, as if the contents of the house had only that morning been brought in by the removal men.

"Everything's always upside-down when the feng shui guy's visited," explained Zak. "I'm telling you, the parents have exploded."

"What's that?"

"Blown up! They're only human beings anyway. They don't know anything, the bastards."

"Mine are back together."

"In the same house? The same bed?" Zak was looking at him in fascination. "How come? Are they doing it for you?"

"Sorry? Did that happen to you?"

"Course. My mother said, 'If you didn't exist I'd never have to talk to that madman, your father, ever again.'"

"She married him."

"I did point that out," said Zak.

"What did she say?"

"That's when the psychiatrist opened his door and asked me whether I'd had any interesting dreams and sexual fantasies and I told him the thing about the fish."

"I don't know," said Gabriel. "Would you like your parents to live together?"

"That's unlikely now, with my dad a queen and all. The kids at school never stop going on about poofs."

"Yeah, it's bad. Still, it's worse to think that we're going to turn out like our parents, don't you think?"

"I've never thought about that," said Zak. "Christ, that's a hell to look forward to. Never marry, I say!"

"Never marry!"

"Just screw and work!"

"Screw and work!"

Zak's place was three times bigger than Gabriel's, with a conservatory overlooking the garden. Gabriel fetched his easel and Zak worked on the script; they both liked the company. At last Gabriel told him that he'd received his first commission, painting Speedy. As Zak was intrigued, later that day Gabriel went home to his room, retrieved the painting of Speedy, and showed Zak what he'd done so far.

Zak stood back from the painting and announced, at last, that the picture was coming up a treat. Speedy looked like a pink poodle who'd won a prize. Gabriel should paint him with a rosette on his chest, or even on his fly.

Later, as Zak read Gabriel the latest version of the script and Gabriel made drawings and notes, a girl walked in, as girls do. Ramona was the sixteen-year-old friend of one of Zak's "steps." She looked as though she could have been one of Degas's dancers. As Gabriel would never be able to address her sanely, he consulted Archie, his own agony aunt.

Archie told Gabriel to close his mouth and be lulling, seductive, kind. He reminded him of something Jake said. "If you become a director, not only will you have the opportunity to speak at inordinate length about the awfulness of other directors, the books you've read and the films you've made, while people listen, because they have to, you will also get girls. Quite a lot of women like cameras, you will find."

Gabriel informed Ramona, "We're making a short film, in the summer. How would you like to be in it—or at least audition?"

Her beautiful lips guarded the tongue of an asp. "How do you know I want to be an actress? Do I look like an exhibitionist? Show me the story and I'll give it my fullest consideration."

"Your fullest consideration, eh?"

"That's right. It better be good."

Gabriel was staring at her. When she left, she kissed him on the cheek.

That night Gabriel and Zak worked on the script until late, writing, making shot lists and acting out various scenes, as well as trying out possible music. When Gabriel felt tempted to dismiss their work as frivolity, as being not-quite-adult, he thought of Lester on his hands and knees on the floor, as serious as anything about a picture and a few words.

In the morning, as Gabriel and his father breakfasted together, Dad tried to discuss his students, which was difficult, as Hannah felt impelled to produce a show. She'd get on her knees and scrub like a martyr at the feet of Christ, occasionally looking up at her employer with imploring eyes. Gabriel had never known her to clean either under or inside anything but now you could have snacked on any surface or licked any crevice. Nevertheless, Dad felt uncomfortable: although he was used to his wife working in front of him, anyone else made him feel guilty. He had remained an egalitarian in theory.

"Thank you, Hannah," he'd say, a phrase he'd heard the upper classes use in films, hoping that this would somehow make her disappear. But she merely took it as gratitude, to which she soon became addicted, following Dad around with a basket full of cleaning equipment, in the hope of more praise.

When Mum came home Gabriel went to her privately and said, without degrading exaggeration, that Hannah had looked after him well enough but that she was no longer as she had been.

"You're right," said Mum. "We're really crammed in here now. She'll have to leave."

"Can't you find her something else?"

"Yeah. I've got an idea. Let me make a call."

Then she asked Hannah to put her best clothes on. As she and nervous Hannah were leaving, Mum mentioned to Gabriel that Speedy was looking for a housekeeper. It was to his apartment that they were going.

"Good," said Gabriel, nodding at Hannah. "Mr. Speedy. I would recommend him, for certain things."

"Is that right?" said Mum. "How come?"

"I've known him for ages. Dad introduced us."

"But why?"

"We were just hanging around there. And . . . I'm painting him."

He had persuaded her not to let Speedy have her copy of Lester's picture, saying he had to have it for himself. She'd agreed, but didn't know what he was doing with Speedy.

Now she stopped and said, "You're doing what?"

He had been afraid of telling her, he didn't know why. It was as if he didn't believe he was entitled to a private life, or that you could keep anything from your parents.

He said, "He looks good, in my opinion. It's coming out pretty well. I'm using a lot of pink and—"

"You've done a picture of Speedy already?"

"Only a little one. It's nearly finished."

"Where is it?"

"At Zak's. Why are you surprised?"

"Nothing, er, funny, occurred?"

"Nope."

"How strange."

"Not really."

She was looking at him. "These things are up to you, I suppose. I don't see why you shouldn't paint Speedy if you feel like it. But why didn't you tell me?"

"You were at work."

"I see." She said, "You're a strong-willed and independent little guy now. That's good. That's how it should be." She opened the door. "Come along, Hannah. I'm going to sort you out now."

Mum was still shaking her head.

When they returned, Hannah looked pleased and started to pack her things. Speedy needed help; he would take her on straight away.

Mum said, "It'll mostly involve looking after his yoga mat, I'd imagine."

"And feeding his dog."

"You've been to his flat?" Mum asked.

"Oh yes. Don't you trust me, Mum?"

"I don't think I have to," she said. "I know from experience you'd never do anything you didn't want to do. Where are you off to now?"

"Zak's—to work on the film."

"Go—go, son, and live."

"Thanks. I will."

Gabriel went to Zak's to look at the picture. Sometimes he sat in front of it an hour at a time, studying his work. He couldn't say the picture was finished but he knew he was so bored with it that he couldn't see it any longer through his own eyes.

"I think it's done," he said at last. "I can't do any more."

Zak helped Gabriel carry it home. Gabriel needed Zak to be there when he showed it to Mum and Dad; he thought they might be less harsh and surprised in the presence of someone else.

Mum and Zak sat at the table talking while Gabriel prepared the picture. Mum had always liked Zak and loved to gossip with him, particularly about his peculiar family life, which she enjoyed comparing to her own.

Gabriel then went upstairs to his father, who was writing up one of his "cases," as he called them. Gabriel had noticed that Dad liked to be called Dr. Bunch by his new students. "Like 'Count' Basie or Dr. Feelgood?" Gabriel had said. "I suppose so," replied Dad, sharply.

Gabriel said, "Dad, I want you to see something. A picture I've done. It's not that great, but it's OK. I like painting but I'd rather make films."

"That's up to you," said Dad. "Whatever you want to do creatively is all right by me. What's the picture of?"

"Speedy."

"My friend Speedy?"

"Yes."

"Where is it?"

Gabriel took his father to see it. Zak and Mum were standing there.

"Here it is," said Gabriel.

Dad looked at it, taking his glasses off, putting them back on, and stepping closer and then backwards.

As Speedy would have liked to have been a star, Gabriel had done the picture in the shape of a wide-screen film frame. It was narrow, a blurred speedy squint or glimpse. In the background, even more blurred, was the busy diner, with footballers, rock stars and waiters rushing through. Lester's picture was in the background, hanging on the wall.

"Not too bad . . . eh?" said Gabriel. "I wanted to get the motion of Speedy and of the place. Do you think—?"

"Christine," said Dad. "Did you know about this?"

"A little," said Mum. "I'm surprised by how much I like the picture. It's great. That's all that matters."

"Forget the picture," said Dad. "I'm not even thinking about that. What about this man . . . Speedy himself?"

"You introduced him to Speedy," Mum said. "Isn't that right?"

"I did. I admit it," said Dad. "I'm happy to introduce him to anyone. I want him to experience the world. You don't want him to turn out like those public school fools, do you?"

"Rex, what are you talking about?" said Mum. "You're going off on one of your mad runs again."

"I'm saying, why hasn't he been doing his schoolwork?" Dad turned to Gabriel and took hold of his arm. "You went to see Speedy behind my back?"

"Rex—" said Mum.

"I want him to tell me the truth for a change. Jesus, things have really gone downhill without me here!" He said to Gabriel, "You don't know anything! A guy like Speedy'll have your trousers down as soon as look at you!"

"He didn't go near my trousers."

"You were lucky, then."

"Dad, what do you think the Religious Education teacher does all day but stick his hand where it shouldn't go? 'The hand of God' we call it. Speedy and I are friends."

"Friends!" sneered Dad. "Is that right?"

"You haven't been at home much," said Gabriel. "You don't always know what goes on."

"That's right," said Mum.

"Maybe you're jealous of me and Speedy talking together," added Gabriel.

"Jesus!" said Dad. He had his hands over his ears. "What nonsense!"

"But Dad," said Gabriel. "Just tell me what you think of the picture! Please!"

"Leave me alone!" said Dad. "I've had it with pictures! I don't understand what's going on!"

Mum was laughing. The one thing she enjoyed was Dad being humiliated, and his consequent anger.

Dad looked at them both and went out in a fury, as he used to. This time, however, it wasn't long before he returned, looking startled and scared.

"What happened?" Gabriel asked.

"They . . . they chased me."

"Who?"

Dad had made it halfway across the pub—and his beloved pint was on its way—when the expressions of his former friends, as they turned to look at him, helped him remember that the last time they'd met he'd shown them the back of his middle finger.

Dad went to the window, crouched down and stuck his head up like a periscope. "Look. Pat's out there. Christ, the bastard's waving! He wants to have it out now!"

Mum stood next to him. "You're terrified. What a couple of tough guys."

While Gabriel and Dad stayed inside, Mum went out and flung bad words at them, which made the men retreat sheepishly.

"Thanks," said Dad, kissing her.

Dad took a final look at the painting of Speedy and didn't mention it again.

A few days later, Gabriel and Zak took the completed portrait to Speedy's apartment, where Hannah greeted them at the door.

"How are you doing here, Hannah?" Gabriel asked her.

"Fridge always full. Mr. Speedy good to me," she said. "He sending me to learn English lessons. But dog is dirty."

"That's the right way round," said Gabriel.

Speedy was waiting in another room. Gabriel had flung a sheet over the picture. He and Zak put it on an easel and Hannah was appointed to pull the sheet down. This was the moment.

"OK, Speedy!" called Gabriel. As Speedy hurried out, looking around wildly, Gabriel cried, "Go—Hannah!"

"Yaaa!" she cried.

There it was.

The real Speedy had his hands over his face; he was trembling and giggling like a girl about to receive her exam results. He put his hands down, went quiet and looked at the picture for a long time. Then he walked round it, as if expecting to see something on the back. They all waited for him to speak.

At last he said, "But my legs aren't quite touching the floor."

"No," said Gabriel. "But . . . they don't . . . they're not always in direct contact with the earth."

"No . . . but you could have—"

"Could have what? Made them longer? The thing is, you seem to fly above it all," said Gabriel. "To me, you skim, right?"

"Yeah. Right. I am a bit of a skimmer, now you mention it."

"Exactly."

"Perceptive."

"Thank you."

"Thank you, Gabriel. Hannah—champers!"

"Wha?"

Gabriel sighed.

They drank champagne and shook hands.

The portrait would be framed and taken to the restaurant the next day.

To celebrate, Speedy would hold a dinner party for Gabriel. "Should I invite your parents?" he asked.

"You should," Gabriel answered. "But let's try and find a date when they're doing something else."

Speedy was laughing. "You are foresighted," he said. "You'll go far."

Seventeen

A few months later the family moved to a new house, not far away. Dad was doing well and Mum was working for Speedy, but it was still only a cottage with a kitchen extension, and a room with a big window where Dad could receive his pupils. The river was near, just across the motorway, and the back of the house overlooked a park. Gabriel had a bigger bedroom than before, with Lester's framed picture—the original: the copies he had gladly destroyed—above the fireplace.

Christine and Rex argued over curtains and wall colors. They had thrown out most of their old furniture and bickered and disputed up and down the Golbourne Road, looking for better old furniture.

Dad often relapsed, falling back into the familiar abyss of paranoia, anger and despair—his "bunker"—if anything painful occurred. But he couldn't sit in it for long, as he had to teach. Even if he found himself inexplicably hating some of his students, working always changed his mood. He said it had been years since anyone had asked him the sort of questions his students did. Every day he had to think hard, which he found a pleasure.

Mum and Dad were in a hurry now, relatively; there were places they had to be. Dad traveled to colleges and theaters around the country, giving "workshops" and watching how people learned, even as he taught. He kept saying he wanted to write a manual called *How to Listen*—or *What Your Ears Are Good For*—for which he made notes constantly. Neither Gabriel nor Mum was convinced that Dad would ever complete this tome, but they wouldn't bet against it either.

At home the phone rang often; Dad's pupils came to the house, mostly after school and at weekends. Dad talked continuously about his students and worried over their progress; however, it was Mum who made him think about where he wanted to take his pupils, musically. He couldn't "improvise" for ever. A little harshly, she also advised him not to play his own compositions—"and here's an example from my own work"—to his guitar students. Not that he gave up writing music: he was planning to produce his opera with students, when he had time to finish it. He was, at the moment, thinking about the soundtrack to Gabriel's film.

Mum and Dad were both working but went out more than they ever had. At first Jake gave them tickets, as he was invited everywhere but was too busy to go. Mum loved dressing up and, besides Jake's invitations, persuaded Dad to go to the theaters and galleries, concerts, exhibitions and restaurants recommended in the newspapers. If Dad was busy, she took Gabriel.

Mum and Dad argued, but they seemed to be "for" one another in a way they had never been before. The two of them were together in a restaurant when Dad got down on one knee. Mum thought he'd dropped a dry-cleaning ticket, but he was proposing. When she was able to stop laughing, she agreed to marry him.

A few weeks later, on the way to the registry office with Gabriel in his best clothes, she kept saying, "But I'm not sure, I'm not sure."

"Nor am I," said Dad.

"We'll never get there without killing one another!" said Mum.

"Shut up both of you," said Gabriel. "You deserve one another."

The wedding was attended by friends, relatives and Hannah, with a party thrown by Speedy in a room at Splitz. Everyone who mattered was there, apart from Archie, who came in spirit. Zak was amazed and furious with envy. There weren't many kids who got to attend their parents' wedding. Speedy had set up some instruments on a dais, and Dad and his friends played tunes from the old days, everyone dancing until the morning.

When the summer came, Gabriel found himself behind a camera for the first time. He and Zak were about to start shooting the movie's first scene, set in the local market. Ramona was weeping with fear in the clothes Mum had chosen for her, including a pair of high-heeled strappy sandals. Hannah was an extra, shopping in the background and smiling at the camera, as if people back home could see her through it. Carlo was doing the sound, and a couple of Dad's other pupils were helping with the lights and equipment. Gabriel would edit the film at Jake's house, on his equipment, with Jake overseeing everything.

At last Gabriel looked through the camera and saw the first scene as he had imagined it. He had rehearsed; the light was ideal and everything was in place.

Archie was calm within, steady and encouraging.

This was the only kind of magic Gabriel wanted, a shared dream, turning stories into pictures. Soon the images would be on film; not long afterwards, others would be able to see what he had been carrying in his mind, these past few months, and he wouldn't be alone any more.

He checked that everyone around him was ready and raised his arm.

"Turn over!" he said. "Turn over! And—action!"